YORK
LITERARY
REVIEW
2021

EDITORIAL BOARD
Amy Boyle, Catherine Gent, and Lily Smith

MANAGING EDITOR
Seline Layla Duzenli

First published in 2021 by Valley Press
Woodend, The Crescent, Scarborough, YO11 2PW
www.valleypressuk.com

ISBN 978-1-912436-70-5
Cat. no. VP0190

A CIP record for this book is available from the British Library.

Contents

Foreword • *Dr Rob O'Connor* 5
Preface • *The Editors* 7
1069 • *Peter Arnds* 9
The Funeral Coat • *Chris Bailey* 17
Rebecca's Boathouse • *Anna Boyle* 22
Postcards to William • *Beth Brooke* 24
overgrown memories • *Elinor Clark* 26
Tattoo • *Shelley Corcoran* 27
the coming of looked-forward-to things • *Lucy Crispin* 28
darling you haunt me, but tell me do i haunt you still? • *Tash J Curry* 29
Fishing for Iron • *Joseph Darlington* 30
On Hawthorn Ridge • *Sarah Davy* 34
coming on spring • *RC deWinter* 37
Each Time There is Lightning • *Peter J Donnelly* 38
A Piece of Coral • *Scott Elder* 39
Crosby Beach • *Nathaniel Frankland* 40
When We're Apart • *Jeremy Gadd* 42
Passports • *Victoria Gatehouse* 43
Siren • *Elizabeth Gibson* 44
Keeping Watch • *Daniel Hinds* 48
As Beautiful Things Always Do • *Neil James Hudson* 49
Was I there? (Memories, lies and half-truths) • *Beth Kilkenny* 52
In the Shed • *David Linklater* 59
Straight Talk • *James McDermott* 61
Mechanics of Family • *Lucinda Morton* 63
Physics of Mourning • *Alicia Sometimes* 65
Anniversary • *Claire Urquhart* 67
The Butterfly Effect • *Cheyenne Uustal* 68
Camouflage • *Lydia Waites* 72
An Elegy for a Box • *Emily Walker* 74
first memories • *Carl Walsh* 76
Quiet flows the Hull • *Clint Wastling* 77
Whalebones • *Indee Watson* 78
Returning Home • *Lorraine Wood* 80
Author Biographies • 85
Acknowledgements • 94

Foreword

'Time and memory are true artists;
they remould reality nearer to the heart's desire.'
– *John Dewey, American philosopher and education reformer*

PEOPLE ARE ALWAYS saying that 'time flies'. In the past tumultuous year, I have preferred to think of time not as flying, but as something that is mysteriously fluid: at one-point memories immerse us entirely, stretching seconds into hours; but then hours, days and weeks become lost in a momentary glance. This is the intrinsic connection between time and memory. Present and future time are manifested from the units of time that have come before: seconds build on seconds, minutes on minutes and so on. The present and the future are directly connected to the past, where memory also resides. Time is born and instantly becomes a memory. Conversely, memories are dependent on time, that recollection of action, space and people in a specific moment. A certainty we have in our minds of how things were, who was there, what was said. Yet, as is the problem with history, do we paint an accurate picture, or just recall the reality as we wish to remember it?

The pandemic has done strange things to time and memory. Collectively, as a nation, we have yearned for 'the days before' – a now mythical time without the threat of Covid-19, where people gathered, hugged, made memories. It is as if the growing threat eradicated memories and disjointed time. I have heard people refer to 2020 and 2021 as 'the years that time will forget' or that those years 'don't count', as if our ability to form memories is dependent on intimacy and contact.

However, I firmly believe that this is not the case. The nature of time means that not only has the pandemic been a global experience in the present, but it will also become a shared, global memory. This is where the hope resides. We will remember this time for the rest of our lives, these memories changing us forever. Yes, there has been some terrible times of collective and individual loss, but there have also been moments of joy: new life, new starts, new jobs, new homes, new loves. The world has continued. Time has moved forward and new memories have been created. We have just had to seek them out. My hope is that when we look back on this time, we will choose to focus on the positive memories, those moments of human kindness, human endeavour, human strength. Realise that by remembering, we can move on and prevail.

The work in this collection is a testament to the power of time and memory to shape our identities, showing how both memory and creativity can see us through the darkest moments we experience during our time in this world. It is by appreciating time and residing in memory that we can begin to understand and treasure our own existence in the cosmos, to craft the universe in any way we desire. By doing so, we can get through anything.

Read on and remember. You are all masters of time.

Dr Rob O'Connor
York St John University
York, June 2021

Preface

DEAR READER,
We are excited to share with you the York Literary Review 2021!

As a team based in the heart of York, we were keen to add to York's literary history. Having lain dormant for two years, as part of our MA Publishing course, we decided to revitalise the York Literary Review for a contemporary readership.

When thinking of a theme for the 2021 edition of the York Literary Review, we knew we couldn't ignore the current global circumstances. But, we didn't want to focus solely on the negatives. This led to this year's theme of 'Time and Memory', which we hoped would encourage people to reflect on past experiences and look forward to the future. Just as the rings of a tree stump speak of the past and the growth it took to get there, we hope this year's anthology will consider where we have come from and where we will go.

From this, we received everything, from stories of fishing in the river Ouse to a query on the changing of the self over time in a bar in Germany. Most of the writing submitted was hugely positive and provided a hopeful sentiment that was refreshing to read. The variety of pieces has resulted in a wonderfully eclectic anthology that we are certain will intrigue and interest all who read it.

As a team dedicated to equal access to publishing and in support of the growth of Northern independent publishing, one of our mission statements was to showcase the work of Northern writers. However, York itself is a city of multiplicity, and so we were equally keen to highlight this. Therefore, the final anthology is a collection of writing from those closer to home and those further afield, which we believe acts as an accurate and pertinent reflection of the city we are home to.

We hope that our anthology provides a glimpse of hope for the future amidst a current time that has been largely static. We have loved working on this anthology and can't wait for you to read it!

So, sit down with a cup of tea (Yorkshire Tea, of course), and enjoy!

The Editors,
Seline, Amy, Catherine and Lily

1069

Peter Arnds

I observed his languid approach from my bench seat outside the Irish pub on Karl Liebknecht Strasse, a street previously known as Adolph Hitler Strasse until it was renamed for a socialist party leader by the Soviet forces that occupied Leipzig after the war. The man was limping slightly and looked to be in his mid-sixties. As he passed by his cane connected with the leg of my aluminium chair and he muttered a word of apology in German.

'No worries,' I replied automatically, the phrase slipping out in English as I dug into my dinner of Irish stew. I sensed his abrupt stop, knew he had turned to inspect me, and predicted the question long before it came. 'Are you American?' he asked.

'German, actually, but I've been living in the States for the past fifteen years.' He came right up to me then, close enough that I could see how careworn his clothes were.

'You're like me,' he said, 'except I'm an American living the last fifteen years in Germany, right here in Leipzig.'

In normal times I would have simply smiled and then gone back to my food, but I found myself motioning towards the empty chair at my table out of a sudden urge to be social. He shook his head. 'No money,' he said, then reflected. 'But, hey ... would you buy me a beer?' After ordering his drink he asked where in Germany I was originally from, which can never be answered easily. He listened politely to my long list of places I'd moved between as a child, then leaned forward once I'd finished and held his hand out to formally introduce himself.

'My name is One Zero Six Nine.'

'Sorry, say that again?'

'1-0-6-9' he repeated, drawing each number in the air as he spoke. His Guinness arrived and he filled the awkward void in our conversation by giving grief to the waitress. 'Hey Moira, where's the clover leaf on the foam?'

'Not your lucky day, OneZero,' she laughed, jotting down his beer on my tab.

'That's my nickname, by the way,' he said. 'Just the words One and Zero, all together, no space. And thanks for the beer.'

There was no option but to ask, 'Why numbers?'

'Why the hell not?' he spat back, clearly annoyed, but he curbed his anger quickly. I hadn't paid for his beer yet.

'So why those particular numbers? One, Zero...' I tried again, leaving the question half-finished. How could anyone want a nickname that suggests your life has been a failure. Was he a new-Age spiritualist, a masochist, or was this just his odd idea of a joke? He eventually answered.

'Do you think that when our parents call us Mike or Jim or Melissa that we can be as unique as when we call ourselves by a number? A number can express infinitely more than a name. Let me tell you what the One in my name stands for –it embodies my personal conception of nature. Do you know the line?' He quoted Whitman's 'Song of Myself', 'I celebrate myself as one individual among the various forms of life. As a single entity amongst millions of other entities, animate and inanimate. But yet, even though I am an entity unto myself, I am part of the whole of life which is one. I am one; life is one, and together we are one.'

'And the Zero?' I asked.

'Time! It is all about time. The zero reflects my relationship with time throughout my movement through life. A zero perfectly recognizes the past, an openness to the present, and it demonstrates an awareness of the future all with equal regard. I am in all three time zones at once, starting and ending at zero with respect to my march along the timeline of life.'

He sat back and took a long sip from his beer, as if he'd just made everything clear. 'Isn't life complicated enough?' I asked.

He chose to ignore that question.

He had been transforming into 1069 for twenty-five years, he explained, and it had been an extremely tedious process. At one point, 'in a different line of time than this,' it had taken him to the highest court in the land.

'The U.S. Supreme Court,' he said, 'does not accept the argument that a man has the right to turn himself into a number. So I came to Leipzig right after the Wall fell, at a time when this was pioneer territory. The newly opened East. Back then a man could still be just a number. Nobody ever messed with me then, but it's getting more difficult now.' We drank in companionable silence for a little while, until I decided to destroy it.

'If we're talking about time,' I said, 'you don't have to go too far back in German history to get to the part where Jews were no longer identified by name but by number, one assigned them and then inked onto their skin after they entered the camps.' He chose to ignore this observation too, so I tried a different approach. 'What is so unique about being a number? Aren't we identified by enough of them already, at least in the eyes of the government and corporations? Phone number, employee number, frequent flier miles, customer loyalty points, bank account number, ATM pin code – I've got too many numbers to even count. Way too many to ever remember.'

'Not me,' he said proudly. 'Got no time for any of that.'

'You must have a Social Security Number, being from America.'

'Left that back in the States. Have nothing here, not yet. This is the wild former East!' he thumped the table for emphasis, startling several friends of his who had slowly been joining us. Claire from Cork, Mark from Sydney, Andrew from Inverness, and some others. All of them mid-thirties, all expats from the English-speaking world. I forgot most of their names within minutes of being introduced.

More friends arrived, grabbing up the free chairs from surrounding tables to sit with us and antagonizing every nearby German as they went. The intense stares aimed at our group were equal parts hostility and curiosity. I kept moving my own chair, ever insistent on the amount of personal space I had gotten accustomed to over years of living in the open expanses of the American West. The expats chatted away happily, their relationship with 1069 one of indulgence and fondness. He occasionally returned their affection with a sideswipe of bitterness.

'Look at these losers,' he said to me, leaning slightly over and into my sacred realm, 'they are all single. All of them. How about you? Are you single?'

I told him I wasn't.

'Any children?' His eyes seemed to have acquired a slight watery sheen. 'One son. He's seven.'

'Where in the States do you live?' he probed further. I was starting to feel uncomfortable but I'd invited him and his friends in and so I was expected to offer myself up to a natural amount of inquisition.

'Kansas.'

He sat back suddenly, finally exiting my personal space. 'Seriously? Kansas?! You're a pioneer, like me. My frontier is here, the previously closed East. Yours is wide-open, the Great Plains.'

A pioneer? Perhaps. I felt more like a prisoner at times. I'd heard what was coming next all too often and had internalized it over the years. Kansas is situated at the very bottom of the list of places people pick to visit on purpose. It's a 'pass-through' state, where signs advertising five-legged cows and the World's Largest Prairie Dog rarely succeed in enticing drivers away from the interstate. Known for being flat and full of cornfields, in truth, it has gentle hills and soybeans are its primary crop. It had become my personal place of exile, somewhere to hide out while life was happening elsewhere, as in the way it was happening right now on Karl Liebknecht Strasse.

'What do you do for a living?' one of the expats wanted to know. His name was Moses, and he'd already mentioned he was a non-tenured research assistant at the local university.

'I teach German,' I mumbled. Over the years I had learned it was best to be quiet about your job title as an academic. On the other hand, I didn't want to dish up a lie now and be forced to spin my vague answers into a longer story that could easily collapse as the evening progressed.

1069 was not one for understatement, however. He'd only taken sips from his Guinness but it had made him grow loud. His veins seemed to flow with equal parts booze and blood, and it seemed the foam alone was enough to send him back into the pillows of inebriation, wrapped up comfortably in a blanket of sudden self-confidence. 'Wait, so you're a professor in Kansas?' he yelled, more as a statement than a question. 'Hey everyone, we have here a German who teaches German to American farm kids in the middle of the Midwest.' This caused puzzled-looking Germans at the surrounding tables to pause mid-conversation, their stares purely curious now. 'Do you have tenure? Are you a *Beamter*?' 1069 asked, pronouncing the German term for safe and cushy civil servant jobs as if they were something he wouldn't touch with a ten-foot pole. Yes, I was tenured, I said lamely, thinking that my new expat friends seemed to be silently reassessing me over their drinks.

'Did you hear that? He's got a wife. A kid. He's a tenured Professor!' yelled 1069, who was now in tremendously high spirits. He addressed his friends as if they were his children, nearly knocking over his cloverless Guinness. Turning back towards me he put his hand on my forearm, pub air travelling on his breath. 'You've done the hard work, my friend. Be proud.' He tried then to whisper, failing poorly. 'Look at them – all single. They shy away from anything that takes time and commitment. But you're a man with responsibilities!'

'Hey, OneZero,' said Andrew, 'did you tell the professor the real reason for changing your name?'

'I might if he buys me another beer.'

I agreed on the condition that he stop exuberantly praising my life's achievements. I tossed out assurances that my job wasn't all that ideal, that I was a lonely and solitary soul, even with a wife and child. As soon as I made friends in Kansas I was in danger of losing them again because people were always trying to leave. Nobody wanted to die in some small Midwestern town. No one wanted to spend their entire life in a place known for being flat and empty, where any tourists who did come stayed only long enough to look for a fictional yellow brick road that was supposed to lead them right back to someplace more interesting and exotic. Sure, I joked, Kansas is paradise – if you're seeking the peace and quiet of the afterlife. Nightlife, on the other hand, is what you move to a city like Leipzig for, to drink with strangers from different countries in trendy bars on a street so old it's been named after Bishops and Kings and a fascist Dictator before it eventually settled on being Socialist.

None of these arguments seemed to impress 1069. 'Don't you like it there?' He was surprised by my lack of gratitude as an immigrant who'd found success in America. 'I do,' I said, 'but I miss my home here.'

He shook his head in disbelief. 'Stay in Kansas. It's your duty. It's a rewarding job. Fate has been good to you.'

'Do you live on Karl Liebknecht Strasse?' I asked, mostly to distract him from me. His enthusiasm immediately dipped.

'I'm transiting through time,' he said, seeming almost completely sober again. 'Surely you have a place to stay?'

'I live in a truck.'

'A nomadic lifestyle, pure pioneer style,' I replied, trying not to sound facetious.

'It's a style,' he said, his voice firm. 'Let's just call it a style and leave it at that.' Our pints of Guinness arrived, his once again without a clover leaf while mine had one imprinted deep into the foam. I wanted to swap so he would not have to pick it up with Moira again, but he had no interest in trading drinks.

'It's fate, Doc, don't you see. Fate is not on my side, it's on yours. We can't swap that.' As she updated my tab he said, 'Moira, honey, one day you're gonna bring me a lucky clover leaf. That'll change my fate. I'm sure of it.' She left the table with a little laugh. 'Hey, Doc … how long did it take you to get your PhD?'

'My doctorate? Three years.'

He seemed surprised.

'I had a three-year scholarship, so I didn't have to do much student teaching. I made sure I finished before my funding did. Nobody thought I could, but I worked like a dog to make it happen.'

'Let me shake your hand for that.' His handshake was like mud. 'Congrats, Doc. You wrote a dissertation in that time too?'

'Sure,' I said, and not without pride, having momentarily forgotten to cut a low profile. 'Much respect. I was there once, you know.'

'Where?'

'At the dissertation stage. I was a graduate student too, in another line of time.' 'What happened?'

'He never finished,' said Andrew with a smirk. The highlander had a distinct edge to him that made me restless. 'His wife and kids never forgave him.'

'You have a wife and kids?'

'Had. He had a wife and kids.'

I ignored the Scot.

'Did your wife leave you because you didn't finish?'

'The other way round. He left her.' I wished Andrew would shut up and let 1069 speak for himself, but he'd become silent.

'Where are they now?' I wanted to know, emboldened by my Guinness and German directness that often led me to ask questions Americans considered too personal or impolite.

'Who?'

'Your wife and kids. Have you kept in touch?'

'My wife's up there,' he said, pointing at the clouds over Karl Liebknecht Strasse, 'but we don't talk. The kids are in Minnesota. We also don't talk.' He drained the rest of his glass. 'Buy me another one, Doc?'

Claire was worried about him. 'You drank that one fast. Have you maybe had enough?'

'I think that is up to the Doc to decide.' His voice was back to full volume.

'Ok, one more,' I said, sending Claire a shrug. She looked at me reproachfully. 'Why don't your kids talk to you anymore?'

'Not the most intelligent question, Doc. Not for a Professor.

I left them, of course. Hey, Moira, one more. She is my personal goddess of fate, you know.' He winked at her, and she gave him a laugh.

'How old were they?'

'Who?'

'Your kids. How old were they when you left them?'

He looked at me for a long time then, unblinking.

'My son was almost two, my daughter three.'

We both fell silent until the Guinness arrived again. 1069 traced his fingers along the glass, caressing it like a lover.

'Did you get a clover leaf?'

He was deep in thought and hadn't heard my question. When he finally spoke again, it was to ask me to take my glasses off.

'Why?'

'I want to put them on.'

'Never! I never give anyone my glasses. I'm basically blind without them.'

'Come on, let me see through them. Just once.'

'Leave the man alone,' said Claire, who had taken on a motherly tone as the night progressed.

'I just want to see what things look like through the glasses of a tenured professor.'

'I'd rather not,' I defended myself. 'I don't hear so well without them.' That seemed to amuse him greatly. It fit perfectly into his world. He didn't ask why. He didn't need to.

I explained it anyway, so that the rest of the expats would understand. 'When I take my glasses off,' I said, 'I step back into my own world too much. It makes it impossible for me to relate to anyone else. I have to be able to see the people I talk to, otherwise I can't hear them.'

'You're a strange one, Doc. But, I like you.'

He went into the pub to relieve himself then. It had grown late, and I had a long way to walk still, almost to the monument commemorating Napoleon's defeat at the Battle of Leipzig in 1813.

'Just a minute,' 1069 said when he arrived back to find me putting on my jacket and saying my goodbyes. 'I want to show you something.'

He accompanied me down the street a bit.

'Isn't this beautiful,' he said, 'an evening like this one. Time well spent, Doc. You've brought us all together. Isn't it great how our stories collide and mingle? A spontaneous combustion of personalities.'

He produced a worn-out billfold and started digging around in it, though it held only tiny pieces of paper. Suddenly he was holding an old credit card up to my face. Quickly flipping it around he pointed a finger at his signature. In a complicated flourish, he had entered the number 1069 in the white space where his name should have appeared, with the 10 so large that the 69 had withdrawn inside the zero almost to the point of indecipherability. But I understood it too late.

I'd missed my *Augenblick*, that literal blink-and-you'll-miss-it moment in which I could have read his real name engraved on the front of the card. Later on, walking down the quiet end of Karl Liebknecht Strasse, I realized that moment had been the most intimate of the entire night, a gesture 1069 had felt he needed to make. He had offered me a rare glimpse of who he'd once been, 'in a different line of time than this,' before he'd tried to redefine time and transform himself into a number.

The Funeral Coat

Chris Bailey

By the time I really started to know him, my Granddad had a funeral coat. That hadn't always been the case, but now he was of an age where his smart, charcoal-grey, woollen coat – his 'coat for best' – only ever saw the light of day for funerals. Usually those of friends, family members, ex-colleagues and church members. He would open the wardrobe in his bedroom and, with an automatic slice and drag from the back of his hand, slide the clothes along the rail a little way, so that he could pull the coat out on its hanger without stretching the long, clear polythene bag that kept it in pristine condition. The wardrobe door would stay open until he came back from the wake and put the coat back in its same place, replacing the polythene bag as he did so. Everything in my Granddad's house had its right place.

This time, as he got his coat, I stood in the doorway of his bedroom, examining prints of paintings of tall ships. Paintings full of white water and perilous journeys, painted by romantic men dreaming of adventure and glory. I asked him, 'What's the occasion?'

'Sally's funeral. Do you remember Sally from church? She used to sit behind us, always wore the hats? She was a lovely lady.' He paused on these thoughts.

His Liverpudlian accent, softened by forty or so years away from the city, would always push the emphasis on the superlative adjectives. She was a *lovely* lady. It was never insincere. He was never an insincere man. He was kind, generous and warm. His disappointments always gave way to forgiveness and unconditional love. He was, to me, as close to God as I had ever felt. He was the kind of God you read about in Sunday School. Not the God I had come to know since; cold and dispassionate, yet paradoxically vengeful and malevolent. Nor the God I had abandoned as I hit my teens; a preening and demanding God, expectant of worship and adornment, but a *good* God. A gentle voice, and a guiding and protecting hand.

'She was a lovely lady.' He said again, his old, creaking voice, softening the vowels as the words wrapped around me.

The tall ship paintings hung in fake gilded frames on the walls.

A strange textured wallpaper that resembled hessian acted as their backing. It was around the whole room. Had the window not been so big, it would have made the room look dark and quite unsettling, but as it was, you could only really tell when you looked quite closely. That window looked out to the main avenue in a council estate that had been my home growing up. I hated the place. If it wasn't for him, I would have never gone back at all. My Granddad – Joe – put on the coat. His movements were laboured and accompanied with the low moans and groans of old age and arthritic joints. I moved from the door frame of the bedroom and sat on the bed as he slowly passed me. 'Are you going to be too hot in that?' It was May. 'No. I don't think so Son. My bones are a lot colder than yours these days.' He paused between each sentence carefully, then smiled at me and went downstairs to wait for his taxi.

He had called me Son for a long time. My uncle, his son, had died a decade or so earlier from a completely freak epileptic fit. In an instant, he asphyxiated in his sleep. The coroner said there had been no pain. No suffering. Perhaps that was true for my uncle, dead at thirty. For everyone else, the void was incredible. An emotional Grand Canyon appearing in an instant. A fissure that made the grief feel physical, geological; it would weather, and possibly even erode over time, but it would never be filled in. A scar on the landscape of our family. To anyone else; another small, polished granite stone in a cemetery on the edge of town, with another name they wouldn't know. I don't think my Granddad, Joe, ever recovered from that.

I sat on the bed, considering his words. 'My bones are a lot colder than yours.' Downstairs, a familiar double click of the latch as he pulled the door shut behind him. 'These days.' The faint slam of the taxi door and the pause before the acceleration took the cab away from the house and everything went back to being silent. 'These days.' It struck me that, at twenty-three, Joe had fifty-five years on me. I didn't know much about most of those years and what I did know, had never really come from him. He had not been a well man for much of his life, and had suffered his share of heartache. I knew he had a quadruple heart-bypass at fifty, before I was born. I knew my uncle was not the first child he had lost. I knew that as a divorced Catholic, he had steadfastly never pursued another relationship. He never tried to fill the gap left by a deceitful and spiteful wife. He had never told me those things. As I sat on the bed, I wondered what else I didn't know about him and I thought about all the things I had never told him about me.

He didn't call me son out of any misguided notions of displacement. It wasn't a psychological coping strategy that began with the death of my uncle. I think that was mostly coincidence.

My uncle died shortly after a long, nasty and fraught custody battle between my Mum and Dad. My brother and I had lived with our Dad since he and Mum had split up. He was a bastard. Everyone knew that. No one had known just how much of a bastard at the time though. A couple years later I popped into the world, followed two years, six months and three days later by my brother. Born into trouble. Innocents suffering the sins of their parents.

When they split, our Mum left in the middle of the night in a taxi. She travelled a hundred miles in that taxi, to my Granddad's house. The taxi driver helped Mum get everything into the car as silently as possible. The black eye and bruises on her arms and wrists were all the incentive he needed to help. As they drove, he talked to her as she cowered in the backseat with her two children. He told her how he was glad to be able to help and how he knew people who could help even more, if she knew what he meant. He told her he would only charge her for the petrol and that he would never tell anyone where he had taken her that night. My Dad knew though. He knew there was only one place that she would go. One place she could go. By the following evening he had driven to my Granddad's and staked out the house until the police and social services arrived. She had kidnapped the children in the dead of night, he said. They didn't take us away from her that night.

Skirmishes came often over the next year or so. Police would be called, social services involved, neighbours standing on the pavement, or looking out of their respective doors and windows, to see the various levels of commotion, threat and violence happening in and around the prettiest front garden on the road.

Eventually, we were living with him, in a council house ten minutes walk from my Granddad's. My Dad had found a house and a stable job. Mum had not. The bruises on Mum's face obviously did not have the same impact on the emergency services as they had on the taxi driver.

Throughout the next seven or eight years, my Granddad would be the resistance fighter in my combative childhood. He was the one who secretly liaised with the school to pay for swimming lessons when my Dad refused to, or would feed us on the way to school because we weren't looked after at home. He would be the one who taught us how to do reverse charged calls from a phone box, so if we ever needed to get hold of him urgently, we could. He was our cold war handler, the one who kept us safe. I think that's why he called me Son. As much as any other familiarity, he was as close to a Father as I really ever had.

When he came back, Granddad was tired. I took his coat, sat him down in the kitchen and put the kettle on to boil. 'I'm going to put this away for you. Stay here, I'll make you a brew in a second.' I took the coat upstairs and brushed some dust off the right shoulder as I put it back on its hanger. It hung lopsided. Something I hadn't noticed before. Something big in an inside pocket on the left side was weighing it down. Reaching into the pocket I pulled out his large wallet. Probably too big for a normal wallet. Five inches across when folded and well over an inch thick. I opened the wallet and thumbed through the wad of fifty pound notes within. My shock escaped as a hushed breath. There must have been over a thousand pounds in the wallet. He had never been a man with money. He had scraped and struggled his whole life. Retired at fifty after a heart attack nearly knocked him into the cosmos, now he got by on a meagre state pension and an equally meagre work one. His hidden wealth suddenly reflected my secret, student poverty. Would he miss one? This was not like pinching a pound out of the change tray. If I could shake my embarrassment to ask him, he would maybe say yes but it would be an awkward moment of schism in our comfortable relationship, a breach of trust from my snooping. As I lifted one of the notes and folded it crisply into my back pocket, I felt a momentary pang of guilt before I closed the wallet and turned it over in my hand. It felt like a mystery. Some kind of clue to parts of his life I'd not encountered before. Joseph O'Donnell the man, not Grandad Joe, or Uncle Joey, or Mr O'Donnell. Something removed, self-contained and private.

Granddad called up the stairs, 'Do you want a brew, Son?'

'Sorry. Just coming. You sit down.'

I put the wallet back where I found it. Inside pocket. Right pocket. Pulled the polythene back on and hung the coat on the railing in the wardrobe.

'Sorry, you had some grass on your jacket. Have they cut the grass at the church?' 'Yeah. Kevin, do you remember Kevin? He's been out this morning doing all the grounds. All the roses are out. It looks lovely up there. Would you like to come with me on Sunday morning? Everyone is always asking after you. Asking how you are, y'know.' It wasn't a trick. He wasn't trying to make me feel like I should go. I think he always felt sad that I didn't anymore, but he just always made sure that he left the door open to me. If I wanted to walk through it, that would be my choice.

'Thanks. I'll see how I feel.' My standard response back. Maybe one day I would go. I finished making the tea and put his cup next to him on the table. 'How was the service?' He pursed his lips and raised his eyebrows in a kind of "so-so" expression. He took a sip of his tea and put the cup back down. 'It was very nice. Father gave a really lovely eulogy. She was only seventy-one. Stroke. I think.' He stopped. 'I do seem to be wearing that bloody coat more and more though.' The funeral coat was a bit of gallows humour. It wasn't that it was tasteless, it was that every time he wore it, it meant he was closer to not needing it. I think that no matter how strong his faith was, that inevitability was never not scary to him. It was scary to me as well. 'Were you too hot?' The opportunity might not come up later, I thought. 'That coat is really heavy.' It was silk lined. Double-stitched. The wallet had thrown me but actually it was a really fine coat. It was more than just a coat for best. Up close it looked, couture. Probably about as old as me, or even older. It was tailored. Hand-stitched. Very expensive. He sipped his tea. 'I don't think I've ever actually looked at it up close before,' I said. 'It's really smart.' He didn't answer at first. He loosened his tie and unbuttoned his collar. 'Would you mind helping me with my shoes? I think I'm just about bushed.'

I knelt down and undid the laces on his boots. I remembered him wearing smart shoes, but these were more functional. Comfort was more important now. Sore bones needed soft shoes not hard Italian leather. 'Thanks, Son.' I helped him to his feet and we walked gingerly into the living room, stopping to put his fleece-lined slippers on as we went. We sat and put the TV on. It was four-thirty. The football scores would be coming in soon.

'Do you like the coat?' he said. He didn't look at me as he said it.

'Yeah.'

'When I'm gone, you can have it.'

We sat in silence and watched as the football scores updated on the screen.

Rebecca's Boathouse

Anna Boyle

A birthday treat, years in the waiting.
A forty-year wish granted at seventy years of age.
A trip to Cornwall, we planned and embarked on.
Du Maurier country, I was well excited, of course!
To Bodmin Moor, our first stop.
Overnight in the Jamaica Inn,
Made famous by the great author;
The pirate ghost that night was not met!

Day one was spent moving further onwards.
St Austell to become our base for now.
Day three dawned, warm, and perfect
For a hike across Daphne's well-worn trail.
Sudden car problems that almost spoilt it,
Were sorted and we quickly went on our way.
To Fowey to start our adventure.
First steps beckoned, Readymoney Cove.

Past the cottage, taking its name from the Cove.
'Hungry Hill' – her first novel was written here.
Ascending high, the cliffs they summoned,
Scent of wild garlic at every step.
Some time later lunch was devoured,
By St Catherine's Tudor Castle high on the cliffs.
Heightened sense of taste was exposed,
By fresh sea air and cloudless sea view.

Onwards, we intrepid duo trod,
The path where Daphne daily strolled.
An abundance of flowers, alpines mainly.
Azure the colour of a clear, calm sea.
Piracy was rife on these cliffs in its time,
Along the rocky shoreline close.
The iron wheel protruding upwards from foam
A sign of a wreck in later years.

Finally reaching Pridmuth Cove and Cottage
Met by a surprise view, stepping out of the woods.
Daphne's life here, swimming each day,
Creating her vivid and fine crafted works.
Beyond this shoreline the murder scene.
Opposite the boathouse where secrets were hid
A three-masted ship, lying now wrecked in the cove,
To become a clue in the thrilling tale.

Significant time spent investigating the area.
And photographs – so many – were snapped in that place.
Another ascent took us above the spot,
Revealed a faultless view to witness.
The final leg, to Readymoney we returned,
Spied a WW2 commemorative flotilla sailing by.
Then a search for Menabilly, Daphne's final home,
A catalyst to future visits, I hope will be very soon!

Postcards to William

Beth Brooke

Coast Path above Eype

The sea calls us;
you are not here to answer.
Ravens, paired, turn and
tumble overhead;
I stand at the edge to watch
the waves crawl,
my thoughts snagging on
splinters of silvered light
across the bay.

Christchurch Meadow, Oxford

The boathouses are shut, the river empty.
The drizzle of late December threatens
rain and only the most stubborn
romantic would want to walk the path;
I am the only tourist on the river bank today.

The Riad Garden, Marrakesh

The evening is soft and warm;
compassionate, it asks no questions.
I watch the moth burst its heart against
the glass of the table light,
consumed by longing for what
it does not know it cannot have.

Hereford Cathedral

Here is the Mappa Mundi – remember it?
The one with Jerusalem at its centre?
It looks to the east for love.
To some it was a chart of navigation,
a treasure map, to others,
a simple relic now, perhaps
of a journey undertaken years ago.

Symondsbury

The pine trees have fruited now,
cones load the branches, heap
themselves on the grass.
I am part of the landscape
beyond what used to be your
window, where the raven
calls its hard, clear song.

overgrown memories

Elinor Clark

up the neat path to the house
   where you had lived long before
      i had lived
    i crane my neck
to see your face   but can't
  it was always overgrown before
     you told me
in a careful voice   as you ran
    your hand along the neat
       line of lavender
   mum   your grandma
was never one for gardening
i nodded   as if i knew that fact
   though not her face
     just a smile and the smell
of microwave food
    digestives   flat lemonade
i filed away the gardening snippet
   fleshing out
     the outline
  maybe in the future
i would mix it with my memories
   claiming it
      amongst my own

Tattoo

Shelley Corcoran

The earliest composition fills me with
a strange type of nostalgia.
I don't recall the pain of needles in skin.
Slight remorse, as with other such
decisions that generate hurt. Nevertheless,
no regret adds up to a life unlived,
or so the tattoo goes.

A reminder of who to be,
what to echo,
how to love, people to forget.

The colour bleeds over the black outline.
A sign of a disagreeable artist
or an indication that being contained
was never an option.

the coming of looked-forward-to things

Lucy Crispin

The coming of looked-forward-to things
can be so strange. They inch towards us,
bearing the dear freight of our longing –
dreams the heart, nursing anxiously, sings
to itself –but then nonplus

us, when they come, with their difference
from what we imagined. For often
it's an abrupt arrival, and tense;
and it's hard swiftly enough to sense
the new place, new things, and to soften

sufficiently to appreciate
the bright-blossomed moment's true fragrance
before –suddenly again –it's late,
and the once-new day closes. The weight
of life drags again, and the soul's dance

slows to a walk, a weary trudge. Though
some moments have, of course, been captured
by the heart's lens –olives trailing low
long garlands over the pool; the glow
on your worn face as you're enraptured

by light and heat and quiet; the sun
riding the sky over morning hills;
snatches of sentences half-begun
and lapsed into laughter: the joy won
from the small things; though this is true, still

we find tomorrow has somehow turned
into yesterday, the future gone,
switched to the rear-view mirror; has burned
its fierce path through us. And we have learned,
oh yes, we've learned, how brightly it shone.

darling you haunt me,
but tell me do i haunt you still?

Tash J Curry

these memories still haunt,
they never falter,
never fade.

they persist seeping
into my dreams,

becoming illusions of the heart.

there's these ghosts,
wandering souls,

for i know they'll never leave,
i exist in the memories of us.

i know time will never
let me be.

that's the price i pay
for still loving you.
but when did i become
a ghost from your past,
living in memories,

reliving nightmares
and calling it healing.

– darling you haunt me, but tell me do i
haunt you still?

Fishing for Iron

Joseph Darlington

My father died outside. Out in the rain. We'd dragged him out there in his bed, the whole family together. I remember I was down by his feet. Tony was up by his head, being the eldest, and Mum, her belly swollen and angry even then, heaved on one side, Katy on the other.

Thinking about it, perhaps he died on his way outside. Maybe he died as we jostled him through the caravan, knocking over lamps and stepping on the cat. Maybe when we squashed him against the doorframe.

He had asked to be taken outside. He wanted to die outside. That's why we were taking him out there. If he gave up and died on the way out then that was his prerogative, I suppose.

All the neighbours gathered around.

'What's he doing out here?' I remember Sandra asking.

'He asked for it,' Mum replied.

The nosy beggars gathered around. It was the closest thing the site had seen to entertainment since the police caught up with Ray Konno, the Bareknuckle King. They all gathered round and smoked and watched. Whether Dad had this in mind, I'll never know.

I was only young then. Fourteen. Katy was younger. Tony, thinking about it, couldn't have been much older than sixteen or seventeen, but then he worked out, and he'd just married Esmerelda six months before that and so he was on his way to being a dad himself. Those things made him seem older to me. Like he was up there with my dad too, an adult.

I remember all the toasts that happened, once we were sure he was dead. I remember the wailing and the moaning. Then, after a half hour or so of sitting in the drizzle, someone or other broke out the moonshine and we started the funeral party, right then and there.

We were all soaked through, of course, but that brought us closer to him. We were all bedraggled, our hair dripping on our foreheads. Whisky, warm in the throat, passed around like medicine. He'd had enough of it while he was dying. Mum, I think, dragged out his half-finished bottle and said, 'Here's to my old man!' and we polished that one off and all.

I'm not one for celebrating a death. I went and sat inside. I surrounded myself with all the odds and sods we'd picked up over the years of dredging.

'Fishing for iron,' Dad used to say, whenever anyone came up and asked what we were doing.

'Interesting,' they'd nod, and walk on.

We went into town. The fishing was better there. The townies made a habit of throwing things in on a Friday night, and had done so for a good thousand years before our magnets came along. We'd find a place, somewhere clear of gawpers, and cast out our magnets. Into the muddy mystery of the Ouse.

There was nothing sophisticated about it. Dad had picked the magnets up from some Roma he'd met at Appleby. Traded them for something, I'm not sure what. Dad never had that many skills. Anything he could do seemed to come natural to every man on the site, which left his talents surplus to requirements.

However he got the magnets, he soon had the idea of tying them to rope and casting them into the canal. That's where it started, you see; the canal just beside the site. He threw them in – *plop!* – the sound of a wet swallow, a big throaty gulp – and then he'd wait a few seconds, letting them get to the bottom, sink into the mud down there, and then he'd drag them in.

After half an hour he'd already recovered the Farleys' old bike, a shopping trolley, two or three old fishing rods and a badge with an official insignia on it that might have meant something to somebody once.

Dad took the things back to their owners. He got a hearty thanks from them and even a couple of quid from the Farleys. I figure that's what gave him the bug.

After he died I sat in the caravan and I looked around at all the mangled old bits of rust that we'd gathered. Things so old and rotten that it was hard to imagine they'd once been objects made by men. Possessions, sitting proudly in people's houses. They were more like weird creatures now, warped by the fairies and turned to stone.

I can't remember when he started bringing them home. It wasn't until later, I don't think.

It might have been after the cough started. Maybe he was hoarding things – something to pass on to us? Or maybe he sympathised with them? The strange, broken down masses of iron, once useful but now rotten, bent, unrecognisable.

Or maybe he just liked them from the start? I don't know. He never said.

Anyway, the caravan was full of them by the end. I sat in between them and looked at them and I remembered all the things we used to catch.

We'd find a place, there on the banks of the Ouse, right in the middle of York. We'd all be there, me and Dad, Katy and Tony. Little Barron was there even before he was born, kicking away in mum's belly as she cast in the magnets. You won't know Barron. He died when he was born.

We'd cast in the magnets and hear the *plop* and let them sink to the bottom. That was the most exciting part for me. I remember Tony would get excited when he was dragging it in. He couldn't wait to see what was on the end. Sometimes, he'd feel something big and he'd get so excited that he'd pull too hard and lose it!

'Dozy bugger,' Dad would call him.

But I was excited when it plopped. Then waiting for it to sink down. I imagined it down there, in the deep. Blind. Heavy. Searching out metal.

Then, when you were sure it was on the bottom, you'd start pulling it in. This is why they call it dredging, but it isn't dredging really. Dredging is what the big boats do down on the Fens, near Kings Lynn, in the East. We went down there to visit cousins once. I saw a dredger. What we do isn't that.

Dad was right I think, we were fishing for iron. It was the same as any fisherman really. You pull it in, slowly slowly, not wanting to lose it after you've got a bite. Then, *wallop!* It's out of the water. You weigh it and you price it and either you throw it back or you keep it.

It was Dad who made those decisions. We'd pass the catch to him and he'd hold it in his work gloves. He'd hold it up to his beady eye and turn it around, like this. Sometimes he'd rub a bit of muck off it or bite it to see how soft it was. Then, after a couple of seconds, he'd know its value.

I think it's only near the end where we started keeping it for ourselves. And it was never anything valuable we kept – only the stuff no one else could find a use for. Only the monsters.

I remember sitting among those strange little monsters while the party went on outside. Dad was dead and gone and back with the ancestors. These were what he left behind. Of all the things to leave, these were it – his legacy.

It could have been the keys we found; ancient things that were meant for unlocking even more ancient secrets. It could have been the fine candelabras or the jewellery. But no, it was these. Whatever they were. I don't think there's a word for them. Monsters is perhaps too harsh. Stuff is too vague. Maybe there's a word in some other language? Who knows? I don't know.

We threw them all out anyway. All those strange things. We chucked them before his body had even gone in the ground. I suppose they never did mean anything, either way. And Dad was not a man of great mystery. A simple man really. He liked being with family, and he liked being outside.

He got both in the end. And now he's in his grave. I still go fishing for iron sometimes but I never catch anything. Not like we used to. Now it's all just rubbish. It's calming though, especially in the drizzle. It's good for reflecting – there with the water and the muck. It's a good place to remember him.

On Hawthorn Ridge

Sarah Davy

I reach into the zip pocket of my bag and feel for the packet. Waxed food wrap, lemon yellow and spotted with bees on lavender, tied with rough garden twine. Hunks of white bread cut into triangles. Creamy mature cheddar in fingernail thick slices. Your sharp homemade pickle with chunks so big I usually pick them out. My fingers hit the bottom of the bag and find dust and a crumpled foil wrapper. I find a patch of grass that is not submerged and set it down to check the other pockets. I unfurl my damp waterproof, my flask and the two pairs of socks already soaked through and changed. My map in its clear plastic cover, binoculars, and my mobile phone. The bamboo box wrapped carefully in a wool scarf. I tip then shake the bag and cat hairs escape the lining, drifting on the wind, and dancing across the moor. The sun is fully out, and steam rises from the sodden ground. My stomach growls, opening and closing like a fist. It is after two and apart from a half black banana on the bus, I have not eaten since breakfast.

The day did not start like this. My plan was simple, laid out in easy-to-follow steps. Take the bus to the foot of the moor, as close as I could get. Then move on foot, about a two hour walk to the ridge with the single hawthorn tree, dotted red and silver against the blue sky. The walk would be easy, a hop, skip and jump to the spot where I would kick off my boots, let sunlight rain down on my bare shoulders and settle to the feast. Our final meal together.

The bus dropped me where I expected. As it pulled away, clouds rolled in and huge drops of rain erupted on the ground around me. The cars that had gathered in the lane slowly disappeared, some walkers turning without leaving the safety of the vehicle. Others drank from flasks and wiped condensation from the inside window to glimpse the view. I peered through the rain coating my glasses. I knew where the hawthorn was, but its gnarled form was clouded in mist. This was a walk I had done almost twenty times. My feet would find their way and my body would follow.

Half an hour in and the rain was filling divots in the earth made by grazing cattle. Every stone lining the way was slick. My feet and legs became disconnected from my brain, taking me left then right until I stopped and realised I was surrounded. Not by open moor and sky but by cows, newly turned out with their calves. Steam rose from their nostrils and one was so close, I felt her hot breath on the back of my neck. The track traced the edges of their grazing land and if you stayed on it, they left you to your travels. The weather had driven me off course. I could not see the edges of the herd but felt them stretch out in front of me, filling every possible way out. My mind raced to find the file on escaping protective mothers who could trample you to death in a heartbeat. I recalled your lesson. 'They can move faster than you think. Do not make eye contact. If you have a dog, let it go – it can outrun them.'

The rain broke and to my left the loose path to the ridge was picked out by a tiny fleck of sun. I dropped my eyes, stretched my arms out by my sides to make myself as big as possible and moved forward carefully. I bumped face first into the dense coat of a brown and white speckled mother. She stayed still. I edged along her, using her heaving girth as my guide. They followed me with their eyes, their heads turning slowly. The sound of grass moving around their mouths and into their gaping stomachs was only slightly louder than my thumping heart. My right hand brushed the tiny damp snout of a calf and I stifled a squeal when I saw it. Bright orange and fluff covered like an orangutan. One of the Highlands. Two more cows and I was past the herd, the sharp stones that mark out the way under my feet. I lifted my eyes but did not look back until I was sure their interest in me had waned. The rain disappeared and clouds were lifting. Thirty odd heads bowed to the ground in daily prayer. I turned and ran.

I do not know how long it took to escape the cows, but it led me off course. What I thought was the path up was in fact the path around. I had to double back via a burn running with earth eroded from the fields and lined with egg yolk yellow gorse that nibbled at my legs. You always said that shorts made more sense, skin is waterproof and dries on its own. Right now, I would rather be wearing soaked through denim than slashed to pieces.

When I finally reach the hawthorn, the weather has gone full circle and the day is as it began. Full of hope and light and promise. But our plan is ruined. I unwrap the box and hold it tight against my chest. The very last breath of you, waiting to be cast into the wind. This was to be our last meal, handwritten in detail with your folio of instructions. No funeral. Just this. Just me and you.

Eating outside was our simple pleasure. Using what we had in the kitchen, sniffing packets and peeling off films of mould to make sandwiches. Stuffing bruised fruit into paper bags, tipping drawers for leftover boiled sweets stolen from hotel pillows. Things we think too basic at home are a banquet eaten on damp grass on a hillside. I spread out my coat and lie back to watch the odd cloud drift by. Wind is starting to pick up and I do not want too much of a breeze when I scatter you. My stomach still grumbles, knotted with hunger and unease. As I shift my weight, I feel a lump under my head. I lift my waterproof and feel for it. Inside the pocket, my packet, squashed flat. I check the other pocket, and find a slim, half eaten piece of chocolate coated mint cake, still in its wrapper. From our last trip to hawthorn ridge. The wind is growing now so I unwrap the package. The bread is flat, pickle has seeped out and the cheese crumbles when I take my first bite. I let it sit on my tongue before my stomach takes over and I devour it. The mint cake's coating has started to melt so when I peel back the filmy wrapper, slithers of chocolate fall away to reveal the ice white sugar inside. It melts in my mouth and I eat it in one go. I need strength for the moments ahead. Steam rises from the flask, strong sweet coffee to wash everything down. You would tut if you could taste it, three heaped teaspoons stirred into the black syrup. Our meal is finished, and I let it travel to my fingertips, let my stomach settle, feel the tingle of sugar trickle through my veins.

When I am ready, I will pack everything away and walk to the highest point, just beyond the silvered hawthorn. The place we met and the place we returned to, year in, year out. I will turn to the wind, open the box, and let you live on here, with the cattle and the walkers and the moss slicked stones, the hawthorn and the wheeling buzzards and the gorse edged stream. But for now, I lie back and let every single bite of our last banquet sing inside my throat.

coming on spring

RC deWinter

the bitter cold snap ended with a whimper
the gentle wind keeping all its secrets to itself
barely disrupting the leftover snow melting
in silent sullen puddles on the cemetery
of the garden where bleeding heart and
cornflowers wait for the summons of spring

> some small feathered thing whispers in my chest
> in a language i feel rather than hear
> a caress on the ribs awakening the ghosts
> of things i'm not sure i can afford to feel
> but would bankrupt myself to own again

sun sparkling on the sea
morning coffee in bed
the gush of love pouring from a piano
eyes shining in candlelight at the dinner table
food a forgotten footnote

> i catch my breath and turn away from the window
> heart beating in the crazy rhythm of hope
> that fickle jewel coming and going
> at its own odd intervals promising nothing
> but possibility and wonder if i too might bloom
> in the greenness approaching

Each Time There is Lightning

Peter J Donnelly

I am taken back to a campsite –
Appleby, a moment of moonlight
in the daytime, it seemed to me
aged four as I watched from the
caravan window. Or a field near Ripon
ten years later – a second of sunshine
at midnight, that lit up the car like daylight
as I walked back to the tent.
I don't remember thunder, or rain,
as there was tonight, before I walked
into the city in search of a takeaway
on the last day of July, after a storm
which hasn't cleared the air.

A Piece of Coral

Scott Elder

There's no charm in this
but I keep it close
    she paused to slip her index
    through a lock of greying hair

one day I'll toss it back
because I, too, am the sea
    she scowled and looked aside

and can only speak of moments
as they move through me
    silence tightened to a knot

in the twilight   a sail-less sloop
inched into the bay   its little piston
a faint throb   an incantation
we listened   blind as thistle

and when came the end
we listened to the wind
as if we were water
or maybe, yes
               the sea

Crosby Beach

Nathaniel Frankland

At some point along
Crosby Beach is where I left it
all –
      (all sense of worry,
          all sense of want?)

the River Mersey the closest of
close confidants…
between me,
my lips,
and the shivering horizon,
not a word was ever whispered to the
wind,
that always swept so deliberately,
from left to
              right
              from right to
left…
no pause for breath as it
buffeted my face,
eyes squinting like venetian blinds in
summer…

…meanwhile,
      as my sense of wonderment wandered,
I negotiated the washed up
      jellyfish…
steadily,
around a minefield of
      pellucid polythene bags…
raw offal
left for dead on the butcher's countertop –
one man's rubbish tip,
      somehow destined to be this man's
        trove of treasure…

like the unruly breadcrumbs in a
half-eaten tub of butter,
(golden gutter!)
       sloping
              down from
                          plastic edges towards the
                                  water –
soft sand stiffening around my feet,
a memory foam mattress
that was meant to remind me of my way
                            back home –
at some point along Crosby beach,
where I used to have it
all.

When We're Apart

Jeremy Gadd

When we're apart I find I'm imprisoned
by a tyrant clock, a dictator of days,
in league with even the crowing cock,
who tortures me with hour long seconds,
and holds me helpless in its hands
and bruises my brain by beating blunt instruments
(the repetitive rhythms of the passage of time).
The worse by far is when I awake,
on the order of an arrogant alarm,
to solitary thought, from sleep's slight respite,
to be reminded, with ticking torment,
of the heartache that's happened since you left,
and the empty pillow where your head has lain.
Then you return, and I that terrible clock disdain.

Passports

Victoria Gatehouse

My back is against the landing wall
as you lift your phone, reel off the rules –
no objects in the background, no shadows,
plain expression, mouth closed.

Looking straight ahead, I'm scrolling back
through the booths of the past –

how my deadpan face, carried
across borders in the pockets of rucksacks,
scanned by security and airline crew,
has altered so little and so much
from that first photograph
in Woolworths,

where I swivelled the chair too high
then too low,
fumbled for the right change,
another slick of Rimmel's *Frosted Rose*,
as I waited for the flash, for my image
to spew forth in four sticky squares,

gingerly extracted by finger and thumb –
snipped out, posted off,
to be returned, plastic-glazed.
Ageless for each decade

and wondering now, how many
renewals I might have left –
how many to be added to the stash
with their corners erased.

Please, ten years from now,
you'll be keeping the shadows from my face.

Siren

Elizabeth Gibson

Remember that night, with the fire alarm?
We were listening to 'Galileo' over and over.
We'd just discovered the Indigo Girls and suddenly our lazy student life had opened out into so much more. Codes, letters, numbers I'd never known about, etched everywhere. We carved our initials in the underside of my windowsill, neatly adding to the short existing list. It was a bay window. I loved bay windows, even back then.

Those winter nights were so brief, a patch of my life that was sad and confused and radiant and can be caught in one scene: you, bobbing about to folk music in the tiny triangle of space between my desk and my wall and my bed. I'd strain in my seat for the light switch, flick us into blackness, press the magical full-screen button. Indigo hour.

Following the flicker of the video's inspirational quotes – at nineteen, we found them deeply inspirational and vowed to live our lives channelling bear cubs and shells and watermelons – we would shudder with how *big* this all was, then look at each other, and swallow, and smile and smile and not be able to stop.

Every time the song ended, I'd say, 'It's gone midnight, maybe we should…'

And you would say what you knew I wanted you to say. 'One more listen, baby.'

And we would listen, and mouth along, and sometimes dare to sing. Quietly. It was barely whispering, really. Like you were hearing my breath, my purest, most basic way of making noise, and I was savouring yours. Your little swallows, your yawns, hiccups. We were dragons who had just discovered they could make heat, make light, and were wondering what else could follow.

My laptop clock wriggled its way to one in the morning, and the radiator promptly stopped humming. I did the usual routine of turning it off and on again, knowing it was unlikely to work this time when it hadn't in a hundred. We sighed and swore this would be the last 'Galileo' before bed. We stood, ready to bop, let loose. In the glorious nineties guitar-strumming instrumental – it began. The siren.

I didn't register it at first, I was so tuned into the song, the little bubble of sound that was important. The outside had blurred out of focus – cars and drunk people. But you stiffened, and I clicked to pause the video. And there it was.

When I was a kid, I was afraid of fire alarms. They were without doubt my greatest phobia. Back at school after every holiday, I would sit trembling, unable to function for the few days before they did the fire drill – and then, once it was over, I could relax, because they rarely did it twice in a term.

Somewhere along the way, maybe at sixth-form, I stopped caring. I can't pinpoint the moment. I just realised one day that it had happened. The alarm was just sound.

Now, I wished the sound would go away so I could lay you down and love you. It wailed on. My hands fumbled with my shoes. I was tired. It never normally occurred to me to be tired, though we got so little sleep. You were holding the door, glancing down the hallway more casually than I would have done. The three of them would be out as usual, I knew that, but my innards churned.

'I'll just close this,' I muttered, hovering and squinting at the YouTube window.

'Hey, leave it, we'll have another listen when we get back in. Whenever the hell that is.'

'No, they'll see it. They check every room. Or they're supposed to.' I frantically clicked off 'Galileo', various other Indigo songs, a Melissa Etheridge. God, I hadn't known I was that obvious.

'And? They won't mind.'

I shrugged, then winced. The draught was already kicking into my shoulders.

We pounded down the stairs then, teeth gritted, out into the icy night. The lawn was sparkly with dew. Our building curved round, not pretty but still a horseshoe, a hug. We jogged through the tunnel of bent-over trees – usually either romantic or sketchy depending on light levels, but tonight just a means to an end – to reach the garden of the older part of the residence. The part we lived in, before we were us.

Gathered below the old building's gorgeous façade, girls grumbled, hopping from foot to foot, some in slippers. In the lamplight, you could see their shadowed eyes, the damp seeping up around their ankles. It was so cold that night.

The alarm whined on. You bobbed beside me in your coat. It was blue and during that period permanently adorned the inside of my bedroom door. When I'd catch a glimpse, it'd make me smile. It meant you were about the place, which was always a happy thought. You nudged me and cocked your head up to the stained-glass windows. 'Remember?'

I sighed and gave you a look to say, 'Seriously? How could I not remember?'

Inside the old building, there were wooden floors where we would dance in our pyjamas and socks. We would wake in our tiny cabins of rooms, and scoot to the showers, the unmistakable smell of girl clinging to every wall and ceiling and floor. We would fly down the labyrinth of corridors to the dining hall, which smelt of history, and we would scrape peanut butter and jam onto toast and giggle as the racket of hungry, bed-headed girls rose up around us. I think that was when I learnt to split the world of sound into two bubbles: everyone else's bubble, and mine – which was just you, me and music.

We would dash to lectures, usually in the rain – this was Manchester, after all – and we would part, and I would wish yet again that we studied the same thing. But when I chose my annoying course, I didn't know that I would also go on to choose non-annoying (most of the time) you. I didn't know about you. Amazing, that I just didn't know you existed in the world.

When I told people where I lived, they judged me, I could tell. Our residence was notorious. All-female, former convent, little and cosy and strict. I was told that parents sent their daughters there to stop them from being distracted.

And then there was me. Kind of hoping to be a distraction to someone.

I felt guilty.

Not about being gay; I was fine with being gay. Mostly. But being gay *there*... You wrapped your coat around yourself more tightly. Your teeth were actually chattering. Seeing you outside and cold at that time of night was odd. You should have been up in the flat with me, snuggled under my lovely purple quilt. It was February, I think. It was cold.

I gave you one of our little signs: just a blink, a tiny nod. You laid your head on my shoulder, managing to make it look friendly. That sort of thing came more easily to you than me. I wonder if our flatmates knew. Sometimes I think they *must* have. If not, they must have thought we were the closest friends ever, having endless sleepovers despite living on the same corridor. We fixed that. We begged. We begged the online system, that is, not the staff. They would have asked questions. I imagine they still probably wondered why we left the old building, that everyone wants to be in, to set up shop in the newer, less charismatic flats.

On the night of the fire alarm, did they wonder how we could bear to stand there, trembling in the frost, faced with returning to a dull flat with dodgy heating and dark, lifeless bay windows, when the old building glowed with squares of yellow and orange, all wooden floors and peanut butter breakfasts? Did they wonder how we could not only bear to stand there, but stand there and smile at each other, occasionally laugh?

Did they notice us at all? We were just two girls in two hundred.

The alarm fell away. Silence. There was a collective sigh of relief, then a bit of awkwardness – that aftertaste I remember from school fire drills of, *oh, the fun's over now, back to real life. Time to drag ourselves up a load of stairs.* Maybe staying put could be easier. Staying out. It would be cold and tough, but with less faffing, less fear. I thought about it a lot, afterwards.

Do you remember?

Do you remember when we were jogging back, keen to drop into bed and cuddle up as tightly as we humanly could and bury our faces in each other, how you turned to me and asked, 'Will you write about this, one day?'

And I said, shivering and joking, 'This was terrible. I want to forget it ever happened.'

But it wasn't true, clearly. Sirens do their job; they lure you out, further and further.

The hall closed down the year after I left – it came out of nowhere, for me, anyway. By then, I was working, and I was venturing out into the city, to bars and film clubs and coffee mornings, and meeting so many people a bit like me.

I don't know where you are, now.

I saw the Indigo Girls live, at the RNCM. They sang, 'Are you on fire?' and, shaking, delirious with the moment, I managed to nod.

Keeping Watch

Daniel Hinds

On the first day of lockdown, I stopped my watch
And hung it on my writing desk.

To slip beneath the wrinkles of Time's face
And sleep within the sandy trench.

I hope I will wake.

I hope I will wake, clamber from my tired bezel,
My sagging gilded case, rise

Like Arthur and sweep the rheumy mist
Of Camlann from my new ancient eyes.

Feel the tickle of my leafy crown, unwilted
By still and silent revolutions.

Touch my startled hand to the thick brush
That covers my face, verdant as the kingdom

My pupils paint, and see the shadow of my graveside
Sundial dialled down to a thin line, hard discerned on stone.

I hope I will wake and find my hands transcribed my dreams
While I slept, my words caught in a willow hoop of ink.

Wake to a collection, two pamphlets and a fat memoir.

On the first day, I stopped my watch
And hung it on my writing desk.

At permanent twelve.

As Beautiful Things Always Do

Neil James Hudson

My sitters were always uncomfortable. They felt like prey, bunching themselves up, looking for exits and generally ruining the picture. This one was different. She hadn't told me her name ('they are easily forgotten') but seemed used to the process, walking into the studio and seating herself on the wooden chair as if she were the artist and I were the one on display. I prepared the canvas and paints, then stared at her as intensely as I could. 'Most people find it easier to look away,' I said.

'I don't.' I was fixing on the bridge of her nose; she seemed to be focusing on mine, as if accepting a challenge.

'Your face is suited to this,' I said. 'Your skin and your hair contrast well. Do you dye it? Sorry to pry, but I'm interested in colours.'

'I like to be monochrome.'

As I stared, her edges began to blur, and I saw an outline seem to detach itself and wobble around her face. I tried to keep my eyes steady as I fixed her onto my retina, but I was disconcerted by her own gaze. I was the one who had to look away, and I turned to the canvas, focusing on the small dot I had placed in the centre. 'That's a nice, strong picture,' I said, looking at the after-image. Colours pulsed in front of me, sharp edges softened into shimmers. I began to fill out the larger areas of colour. Jet black, the negative of her skin, and green where her hair had been; I needed a deeper shade, and mixed it accordingly. I closed my eyes, looking at the images against the black of my eyelids. They looked as if they would never fade.

I had stumbled upon this form of painting by accident. I had been to a small Bridget Riley exhibition, of works from the 1960s. All black and white shapes, swirling and undulating. After studying a mandala, a circular form that seemed to rotate in front of me, I looked away at a blank wall to rest my eyes. I saw a sea of after-images, a negative of the work from my overstimulated retina, an artwork Riley had not painted hung on a wall without an artwork. I sketched the after-images as best I could, noting the colours. When I got home I produced my first after-painting, an inverse of Riley's circles.

'I'll just let it sink in some more,' I said. I stared back at her, allowing her image to burn into my retina. 'What made you want a picture like this?'

This time, she stared down. 'It seemed to sum me up,' she said. 'People don't see me until afterwards. I just fade.'

I wondered how old she was; I had guessed at early twenties, but now she seemed older. Usually I tried not to study the sitter's appearance – I didn't want the real image distracting me from what I saw on the canvas – but I noted that her features were angular and large. This, too, helped with the formation of strong after-images, but it meant that her face hadn't been made for beauty.

I turned back to the canvas, ashamed of being so judgemental. I found I was easily able to wash the colours onto the canvas, smudge the features into each other. I softened her face. Was this what she wanted from me? Strong features were becoming smoother, blurred by the tiny involuntary movements of my eyes. Clashes resolved. When I looked at her I felt a little anxious, but on the canvas there was a feeling of warmth.

I was pleased with it. It only took me half an hour. 'It will need some extra work in the studio,' I said, inviting her to look at it.

She smiled, for the first time since she had arrived. 'It's like a ghost. Or a memory of me.'

'I'm sure you're not a ghost.'

'We're all ghosts to someone. But, thank you. Thank you for remembering me.'

'It will be ready for collection on Wednesday.'

I listened to her footsteps clicking down the stairs. Then I blinked to clear my eyes, and looked at the blank wall.

I could still see her image on it, as if she were painted onto my retina. It should have faded by now, but I could easily make another after-portrait. I carefully took the painting from the easel and set up a new canvas. Her image was strong and colourful.

I began to apply the paint, copying what I saw, making a second portrait in her absence. And this time, I got it. I saw in my painting what it was that her face was hiding. An emotional depth, perhaps, a secret self imprisoned by skull and skin. Something I simply hadn't seen when I was looking at her.

I had no idea why the images weren't fading, but I wanted to keep them. I took out another canvas. I worked quickly, wishing I could drip the colours from my retinas directly onto the blank surface.

I compared the third painting to the second. The colours were fainter, the borders less defined. I was losing her.

I painted nine versions of her, a record of a fading memory. It was dark outside when I finally admitted I couldn't do it any more; that the image on my retina came only from the preceding seconds. She was gone. I wept then, wept her image out in tears that stained my face in green, yellow and red, but even they faded

She didn't come back. I knew she wouldn't; she had wandered away and got lost. All I have is those nine pictures. I look at them frequently, in reverse order. I watch her image strengthen in front of me, watch her solidify and sharpen. She mustn't fade, I'll never allow it. But I can't make her real, and I curse myself. She was right. I didn't see her until afterwards.

Was I there? (Memories, lies and half-truths)

Beth Kilkenny

> 'My mother told the same stories over and over ... if you added them up, there were only about two hours of her life that she wanted me to know about.'
>
> – The Wonder Spot, *Melissa Bank*

Things I remember – True or False

1. Being hunted by a stray dog on Bocas del Toro, whilst in an anti-malarial drug induced hallucinogenic state.
2. Walking the streets of our grey satellite town, in my best ra-ra skirt, clasping a present for a party to which I did not want to go. It was a bottle of peach bubble bath, purchased in the local supermarket.
3. Arriving into Amsterdam by ferry.
4. Nothing.
5. One scene from the movie version of *The Hours* by Michael Cunningham, in which Nicole Kidman played Virginia Woolf.
6. The registration number of the car belonging to the boy I used to traipse the streets looking for. (J419 FNP)
7. Half-heartedly sticking my fingers down my throat.
8. Phones, alive with bad news.
9. Myself.
10. A particularly delicious plate of ravioli in a restaurant off a side street in Rome.

Phones, alive with bad news. (8)

Nothing from my life then remains. Not the people, the house, the job, the neighbourhood. The ties that connected me to her have long been loosened and yet still I remember what we were eating, or about to eat, the night we found out she died. Even though the *we* no longer exists. We were in the tiny ground floor flat, where our upstairs neighbour seemingly had marble tournaments on her living room floor every night. In this tiny two bedroomed flat we had painted our room an awful garish blue, and the spare bed an equally awful playschool yellow, because we were too young to have taste, and we didn't realise.

It was a Wednesday night. I was home in the tiny flat, but I should have been in the Liberties pretending I was grown up enough to be an Adult Literacy Tutor. I had completed the training and was due to have a session with a learner that night, but they didn't arrive. We'd been told to expect this, during the training, that they mightn't show, at the last minute. Still, I was annoyed. You weren't supposed to be annoyed, you were supposed to be understanding. But I had gone there, especially, after work. I waited for thirty minutes or so, and then I walked home, because we were young enough then to live within walking distance of the city centre. Sometimes I do that walk now, except now I walk only to a bus stop which takes me to my house in the depths of suburbia.

What I'm saying is that I shouldn't have been there when the call came, but I was. I was watching TV and he was cooking the chicken stir fry from Supervalu that we used to eat all the time. We said we'd never eat it again. We did. I even eat it now, with someone else. He dropped the phone. It's not something you think actually happens in real life, but I guess when the shock is big enough, it does happen. He was standing in the narrow living room, in front of the fireplace, and I was sitting watching TV so close I'd need glasses if I carried that on much longer. (I did, I do.) The person on the other end of the phone was his sister, and she was calling to say their sister-in-law had died. She was so young. She had a baby. A few days later we were in the kitchen of her family home, and the child was on the floor. He raised his arms up to me and said something that could have been mama. I hid behind the fridge door.

Nothing from my life then remains. Sometimes though in October, when the nights come in heavy and early, and I'm surprised by the darkness despite knowing it would come; those times I remember her.

Nothing. (4)

> 'That was the gift of a short memory. A long
> memory would drive a man crazy.'
> – The Vanishing Half, *Brit Bennett*

One of the things about me is that I have a terrible memory. It's part of our family narrative. Whilst others reminisce about places visited, I might chirp in 'was I there?' Or so I'm told.

I have been alive for 14,786 days. Approximately. Or I mean, exactly, as it happens, as I write this. How many of those days can I remember? Very few of them, in their entirety. Some of them not at all. Many of them, hours, here and there. Maybe there are whole years of which I can remember nothing.

Maybe that's for the best.

The registration number of the car belonging to the boy I used to traipse the streets looking for. (J419 FNP) (6)

I take my daily walk and I'm listening to a podcast about women's bodily experiences. A woman is talking about her experience with infertility. A thought edges into my mind. I don't know yet if it's a memory. When I was younger, say in my early twenties, I had a very short menstrual cycle. Around twenty-one days. A doctor told me I might not be producing any eggs, which I took to mean I might not be able to have children. I certainly had – have – short cycles. Was I really told this by a doctor? Did I spend years of my life as a young woman thinking that I probably was infertile? I can't be entirely sure. You'd think this would be something one would remember. Could I ask for my medical records? What does it even matter now I have two children? The first, a happy accident, by coincidence. Or else, the natural consequence of someone who thought she couldn't have children.

I should switch off this podcast.

The streets I'm walking are those of the suburb I have lived in now for five years. A suburb of a city in which I did not grow up, of a country I moved to as an adult. Five years is not a long time, though it is the longest I have lived anywhere since my childhood home. I never run the risk of bumping into anyone I knew at school, or an extended family member. I don't remember what it used to look like before all the houses were built. I didn't hang around these streets drinking bottles of cider, I didn't spend endless summers walking the streets looking for the boy I fancied. I never bump into myself here. I'm always middle-aged here.

Half-heartedly sticking my fingers down my throat. (7)

Scars are your body's mementos.

- The scar on my chin from when I split it open on the side of a swimming pool in France as a child. For some reason, immediately after the event, I propagated two tales of how it happened and now I can't recall the lie from the truth.
- The scar on my thumb from when I cut it opening a stubborn tin of corned beef. Corned beef, that tells you things, doesn't it?
- The scar just above the knuckle on the index finger of my right hand, from where I got warts frozen off when I was a child. My mother would pick me up from school early to go to the hospital, and on the way home I would get a sausage roll. I remember this time with warmth, despite the liquid nitrogen.
- The scar on the cheekbone below my left eye. At a boyfriend's house, lying on his bed, he opened the window and the speaker fell off the ledge, onto my face. There was rather a lot of blood. He was my first love.
- The scar that I never look at, never touch, but know is there from when I was cut open to make way for my firstborn, whose descent was rapid, and urgent.

That's not a lot of scars, I suppose, for a life. Does my body hold its own memories; is it hiding scars from me? Does it remember the shame I have felt about it? Does it forgive me for the times I ineffectively, and with a certain lack of commitment, put my fingers down my throat?

One scene from the movie version of The Hours by Michael Cunningham, in which Nicole Kidman played Virginia Woolf. (5)

In the film version of Michael Cunningham's book *The Hours,* Nicole Kidman is Virginia Woolf, complete with elaborate prosthetic nose, unkempt hair and, as of then, facial expressiveness. There's a scene where she stands on a train platform and roars at her husband, 'I'm dying in this town.' And I think I've probably repeated that line in my head four hundred or so times since. I don't recall who played Leonard.

Myself (9)

'I no longer value this kind of memento. I no longer want reminders of what was. They only serve to make it clear how inadequately I appreciated the moment when it was here.'

— Blue Nights, *Joan Didion*

I like to throw things out. I find it hard to be calm amongst clutter. I'm forty-one years old and anything of personal value to me is contained within one banker's box. I look through the box whenever I'm trying to find an important document I have temporarily misplaced; a birth certificate, a passport. But I shouldn't be looking there, the bankers box. The box is for memories, not life administration. But I look in the box, knowing the thing I want is not there, and in my hurried frustrated state, find things I have hidden because I do not want to remember. A photo with an ex-boyfriend at the top of the Empire State Building. Sometimes you look at photos of yourself from ten years ago and think *I have no idea who you are.*

One of the reasons I know I am a terrible mother is because I keep very few mementos from my children's early years. It is more important to me that my home be tidy, than that I keep mementos for them to look back on as adults. I don't recognise clutter, as a form of memory, but I can see now that it is. My children have their own banker's boxes; they contain mostly a handful of drawings, finger paintings from creche or school. Some first birthday cards. I didn't keep their baby teeth. I didn't keep a journal of their notable firsts; first word, first step, first haircut. I have no idea what either of their first words were. As it happens, I do remember my second born's first steps, because they were on Boxing Day, or maybe Christmas Day, one of those days anyway. I don't recall my eldest's first steps. Would I have remembered if I had kept the journal? Is writing it down the same as remembering? Or is it cheating? During the pandemic I keep a journal. It is now nine months later, and I am still keeping it, which is the longest I have ever kept a journal. I started it because I knew otherwise I would never remember how it felt to be alive during a pandemic. I don't want to have lived through a century's defining event and not remember it. I don't want to ask, in years to come, *was I there?*

Arriving into Amsterdam by ferry. (3)

We arrived into Amsterdam on a ferry. Is this possible, geographically speaking? It was over twenty years ago. Who knows what's real and what's not from twenty years ago? I remember being on a ferry, and I know we didn't yet have a place to stay, so logic dictates it must have been our arrival.

So, we arrived into Amsterdam on a ferry, I'm almost certain. We had travelled from, I don't recall, some other European city on the student interrailing route. We were doing the trip later than planned thanks to my hospitalisation from an acute attack of what had been diagnosed as ulcerative colitis. I've never had any such severe attacks since, thereby causing me to wonder if I do, in fact, have ulcerative colitis. It doesn't matter, it's not central to my identity or anything, just an anecdote.

Either we had been in Nice, or we would be in Nice afterwards, where, on the beach, we had watched the moon eclipse the sun in the middle of the afternoon and the atmosphere had turned cold and dead, in that way it does when the moon eclipses the sun. The beach in Nice is made of stones; we tried to exit the sea, but each time the tide pulled us back, and the pebbles under foot made it impossible to clamber out, our bodies weak with helpless laughter. I'm not sure I've laughed so much since. It was twenty years ago; I think I said.

Here we were on this ferry, my best friend and I, with no firm plans of where we would spend the night, when we were approached by an older gentleman. No doubt our lack of planning, geographical expertise and knowledge of Dutch shone out of our youthful faces as he asked us, in English, if we needed a place to stay for the night. We looked at one another. We were innocents, my friend and I. Good girls. The man, his name was Benjamin if I recall correctly, produced a book. In the book were testimonies from tens of young people, similarly accosted by Benjamin on the ferry and offered a place to stay. They said things along the lines of, *I know it seems mad to go off with an old man who has just approached you on a ferry but it's all good.* The kind of thing, looking back, Benjamin could have written himself with a few different pens and some creative handwriting techniques. So untroubled had our lives been to date we said yes, to Benjamin, yes, we would like to take him up on his offer of a place to stay, and so we followed him. I don't recall if we walked, or if Benjamin had a vehicle, or how long it took. I do recall, I think I do, that we made that part of the journey in total silence, my friend and I. Each of us presumably contemplating what we would do if Benjamin did indeed turn out to be a psychopath who lured young interrailers to his home. Benjamin was silent too, his English only stretching to an offer of a roof over one's head.

We arrived at the hostel, from the ferry, and were shown to a room where two girls were sleeping. We began to feel slightly less tense. My friend woke one of the sleeping girls, *hey, is this place OK?* With a cranky nod of the head, we were told yes, it's fine, and she turned back over to face the wall.

The next day we took a trip to the Van Gogh museum, with the sleeping girls, although they were awake by then. I made sure to spend a considered amount of time in each room, examining the paintings, reading the details. I would have happily raced through it but didn't want to appear uncultured. I was a young woman on the cusp of adulthood, travelling around Europe with no parental oversight. I enjoyed art. When I emerged into the sunlight, the other three girls were waiting for me. We exchanged thoughts, which can't have been particularly insightful. 'You seemed to get the most out of it,' one of the awake girls said to me. I had got nothing out of it, but I smiled and nodded, that was the effect I had wanted to achieve after all.

You can arrive into Amsterdam by ferry. I googled. Which is to say, I suppose, everything I've told you here is true. I'm sure of it.

In the Shed

David Linklater

I was younger than this
when I looked across the black water
that shimmered with its palm
of lights.

And again as the field became more
but was exactly the same.

Younger when the shed was a machine
flying through time.
Americas in the Walkman.
Canada off on some icy road.
Europe knotted in a flower bed
of cat bones.

Four walls and a ceiling
in my little shed by the shore.
Some candles.
A million thin bicycles keeping me up at night.
Wind chimes impossibly close
to wind chimes down an alley
in Ypres.

It was a museum, a gallery
of wonders
torn down
so another could be built.
And another
that looked upon the same sea,
the same hills blue in their modesty,
the same dreams running over them.

I could cry at the big painting
life has become.

When I look at my hands
they are strange and worn.
I see my father's in there,
my mother's,
my mother's mother.
The freckle on the back
is an island
I've been anchored to.

As with the end of something
comes a start.

That is existence, down to the nails,
splinters and floorboards, and the years
beginning to grip the bones.

Straight Talk

James McDermott

as a boy I
hear your whispers
all of you straight
talking mothers
at the school gate
isn't he a
lovely little
lad and he looks
like he will be
good to his mum
he looks like a
bookish type and
he smells like a
pansy a fruit
he sounds like a
sensitive soul
have you heard him
singing show tunes
have you seen him
dancing around
in those pink shoes
he's found himself
in the closet
he's musical
light on his feet
he's a friend of
the girls love him
one day this boy
becomes a man
wounded by words
he's heard whispered
all of his life
and so now he
works through the hurt
writing it out
in queer poems

which have made him
richer inside
and out this man
is now grateful
to the other
voices to which
he was exposed

Mechanics of Family

Lucinda Morton

My life has run
entirely through cars,
fuel in my blood,
a thrumming engine matching
the flutter in my chest.

Mum's waters broke,
the Mitsubishi
pick-up bouncing,
pulling me towards Earth
earlier than they planned.

The Land-Cruiser
another carer.
Biscuits down seats,
teething rings round the gear stick,
anything I need, found.

The school-mobile
became an Audi,
cool and sleek in
the snow of '04, Polly
Pockets guarding my seat.

Five years later,
the new favourite,
the BMW.
Mum called her Baby as her
real baby grew bigger.

This was the dream,
then my own dream came.
My first baby.
Bright yellow down to her core,
Matilda the Matiz.

More will join my
bright patchwork of cars,
growing with me,
a whole lifetime of engines
to flutter in my chest.

Physics of Mourning

Alicia Sometimes

'We live in a world of unfolding and becoming.'
  – John Polkinghorne, quantum physicist

Time is only a process
        not physically positioned
        in space or in this room
I massaged your aching feet
the lilies spill into the light

Einstein's theory of special relativity
confirms time slows down or speeds up
depending on how fast you move –
relative to something else. I am
completely still, you have disappeared

Time has duration. Our conversations
were endless. They began before they started
        one night you pulled me closer
        to hear your words on how hope
replenished your universe. The shimmer
of your kindness elevating the new moon

Frames of reference help the observer
measure an event. I remember how you
liked your coffee, how your face would tilt
towards the sun but your hands are lost to me
as if they just fell away at the bottom of a page

Time is inside space is inside time:
the dog doesn't know where to sleep
no-one knows where you hid your letters
Gravity forcing me to sit quietly as I try
not to collapse. This weight of grief –
a billion goodbyes at once. Time is not

the barrier, time is only the manner in
which your memory travels back, a clock
face windowless without expression
confirming you are not here
but were everywhere once

Your yesterdays behind you –
            now
                extending in front of me

Anniversary

Claire Urquhart

'If you don't attack the birthday, the birthday attacks you.'
     – Rev. Justin Welby

In the beginning of this ending
I lose myself in a place where my space-time continuum
                                        cannot operate,
Pockets of time between my son's birthday and your death day
Where the syrupy hours cling to the days and dread petrifies
                                        in my gut,
I try to find glimpses of you
But my heavy heart, my black thoughts obscure
All Souls' thin veil

Those eighteen dark days pull me further down each year
Grief and anticipation of grief combining in a brutal mix
I no longer know what I feel from what I felt
Then, four years after your death, I manage to float over
                                        the threshold of these days
Carried in the bubble of new motherhood
I can see flashes of you again

There in the way I peel an orange,
Taught to me because you, at nineteen, decided to learn
                                        Spanish and hitched to Seville
And in how I seek the wind and the waves,
Your gift – showing me their power to reset and balance
There at the end of each day, my default to lock onto the good
Your practice made my habit

And I learn, as I hold my five-day old daughter
On the anniversary of your death,
That there are ways other than tears to mourn, honour and remember
And what you meant when you held me close and whispered
'Love is not spelt Y E S'

The Butterfly Effect

Cheyenne Uustal

It was a building of skeletons. The walls within overcrowded with memories and secrets. The shelves inside lined with displays of items and hopeful treasures that had been collected over time. It was like a miniature museum in the middle of town, but instead of them being precious artifacts of moments in history, they were just unwanted items.

It was a place that I hadn't given much thought about since I was younger. I used to come here every weekend with my Dad and sister. He used to let us pick one item each that we deemed as worthy to be given a second chance at life. Without fail, my sister would moan every time that I was taking too long and asking too many questions. I always wanted to know where the items came from, what their story was and why they were brought here. I didn't understand how I was meant to pick just one and give it a label of more importance over the other items.

But one day we grew up and eventually stopped coming. It all just became a faded childhood memory, until today when it became a welcomed old friend.

The view from my window had lied to me. The sun in the sky and my brightly lit bedroom fooled me into thinking that the spring day had no need for a coat. Oh, how wrong I was. The wind took it upon itself to make me quickly regret my decision, swirling around me and pulling the hairs on my arms up to dance with it. I was too stubborn to turn back though, I refused to give the weather that satisfaction. But all bets were off when the sky decided to pull out the big guns and released its bottled-up tears. The slow drops of rain splattered on my skin, eventually speeding up to make music with the ground.

In the distance the faded 'Magpie's Nest' shop sign swung back and forth as the wind used it as its pinata. But in that moment, it was my saving grace calling out to me like a foghorn guiding a ship to safety. A sigh of relief escaped my lips as I made a beeline for the door, becoming more soaked in the process from the puddle covered concrete.

The closer I got, the clearer the wrinkles of the wooden door became, its pale green paint slowly flaking off. It showed its age once again when it became reluctant to move, requiring me to shove my shoulder into it to jab it awake, taking more green flakes off with me. But soon the sound of the door hitting the bell alerted the shop to my presence as the familiar ancient smell invaded my nostrils.

'Olive? Is that you?', a voice echoed out from the doorway of the back room, disturbing the silence of the shop.

'Mr Hemming!' I said smiling. 'It's so good to see you again!'

He slowly crept out of the slight shadow that the doorway and the dimly lit back room offered him and raised his glasses to rest on the tip of his nose so he could see me better. Mr Hemming was an odd but delightful character. The kind who always had a story to tell. He was a well-known person in the town, easily recognisable with his thinning, grey hair that was always wisping around him making him look like a mad scientist that was continuously electrocuting himself. And no matter the occasion, he always had a heart-warming, gummy smile to offer everyone – the sweetness of his soul clearly visible through his big, dog-like eyes peering at you through his half-moon spectacles.

'Oh my. Well, you have grown up, haven't you? I can remember you when you were about this big.' Mr Hemming crouched down and indicated a height with his hand while shaking his head in disbelief.

'I know, it has been a while hasn't it? It's crazy how quick time goes by without you even realising it. Do you mind me looking around a little? I'm seeking a bit of shelter from the sky's sudden tantrum outside.' My words faded out into a laugh at the end, half from the humour of the weather and half from feeling guilty about not seeing him in so long. But a sense of warmth still bubbled away inside of me.

'Oh, of course my dear! You know you're always welcome here! Stay as long as you like and give me a shout if anything catches your eye.' He let out a sigh with one of his toothless grins, his shoulders visibly relaxing. And just as he was about to go into the back room, he turned to look at me again. 'It is nice having you back here, Livvy.' And then, with a slight nod of his head, his figure was reclaimed by the darkness.

The words hung heavy in the air forcing me to remember all the years that I spent growing up here with Mr Hemming being a significant person in my life. Guilt squeezed at my heart as I offered a small, sad smile to the space that Mr Hemming had just occupied. Why did we stop coming here?

Suddenly feeling out of place, I absentmindedly started picking at the skin around my nails as my feet carried me around the room. Rain dripped down from my hair and clothes leaving a path where I had been as if I was Hansel and Gretel leaving breadcrumbs. A chill hovered in the air – either from the weather or from the ghosts of the items' previous owners. I could hear their salesman whispers trying to convince me to purchase their once loved and precious objects. I felt bad for them. They were forever attached to something that meant a great deal to them, and all they could do is watch as their property sat sadly on the shelves growing duller with each sunny day just waiting to be loved again.

I dragged my finger along making a snail trail in the thin layer of dust that had settled on the shelves as I took in what the shop had to offer. It seemed to have a little bit of everything – music boxes, books, jewellery, snow globes, world globes, photo frames. I wasn't planning on buying anything.

Until.

My eyes landed on a bright red, detective-style trench coat. Maybe I would buy something today after all.

'Mr Hemming?', I glanced around to see his head poking out of the back room.

'Yes dear, is there something I can help you with?'

'I hope so. I was actually wondering if I could buy this please?' I said as I made my way over to him behind the counter.

That same friendly smile split across his face, 'Oh, of course my dear. Yes. Yes. Would you like a bag?'

'Erm…' I peered out of the window to the mist covered world, 'No, I think I'll just wear it, actually. Thank you.'

'Oh of course, don't want you to be catching a cold, do we?', he replied with a slight chuckle. 'Well then, that will be £15.00 please, my dear.'

As I made my way to the door, the beeping and clinking indicated that Mr Hemming was busy putting the money away. And yet I could still feel the mood in the air change. With my hand on the cool, metal door handle, I turned to face him.

'It was lovely seeing you again, Mr Hemming. I'll be sure to pop by again next week.' And there it was – his heart-warming, gummy grin. The mood in the air changed once again.

'Ooh, just like old times! And maybe we could have a cuppa together?' Mr Hemming asked while nodding his head with a hopeful glint in his eyes.

I laughed, 'I would love to!' And with that I re-entered the downpour outside wearing my new coat for protection.

I ducked my head trying to somehow make myself small enough so the rain would miss me. That wasn't exactly going to plan though. I had only been outside for a few seconds and it already looked like I had dived into the ocean. It was as if the rain was out with a vengeance, hating me for finding shelter from some of the storm.

With each step and every beat of rain I could feel myself getting soaked to the bone. I didn't even want to think about the state I was in. I mentally cursed myself for not getting a coat with a hood or even an umbrella. My new, and now completely wet, coat was out of any protection it had. Sky 1 – me 0.

As my last act of defence, I slipped my hands into my pockets in hopes that I could salvage at least some of the warmth that the shop gave me. However instead a cold, slippery object greeted my fingertips. My face scrunched into a frown at the unexpected surprise waiting for me in my pocket. But all lines on my face instantly smoothed out when my eyes finally saw what it was.

It was a photograph of a woman. Wearing this exact coat. Standing there immortalised. Smiling. Waiting for that eternalising flash.

I stopped still in the streets so I could look at it properly, making a makeshift umbrella with my hand so the rain couldn't ruin it. I slowly turned it over to find soft, cursive writing on the back.

Dear buyer,
The coat that you are wearing once belonged to our mother who is unfortunately no longer here to use it. She'd be so happy to know that you helped the coat live on. Thank you.

I smiled and looked up to the sky to send my appreciation for the photograph and the note. Something inside of me felt grateful and fulfilled. The curious, little girl in me smiling. I even thanked the sky itself for sending me into that shop today.

It's amazing how one small action, like going into a shop or buying a coat, can impact so many other people. A small act can make someone's day without you even knowing it.

Camouflage

Lydia Waites

It brings to mind soldiers and hunting. Or the fish you see on nature shows that become just another layer of sand on the seabed, the kind I search for and startle at when they stir. One second a fish, the next a portion of coral reef.

Camouflage.

Derived from the word *camouflet,* a whiff of smoke in the face, it is deception, disguise, survival.

It is also the pattern I wore, inexplicably, for a year of my childhood.

* * *

That year – recalled by family and friends as my camouflage phase – was a study in contradiction, those colours designed to blend in making me a sore thumb. Not a means of concealment but a protruding patchwork of greens and browns adorned with the unmindful confidence possessed by children. *Here I Am.*

Only when I wanted to blend in did I shed those layers. The shoes, the wristwatch, the heavy jacket and trousers with more pockets than I had possessions. Even the military lunch box vanished overnight, replaced by some featureless tupperware. It would be some time before the tomboy years bracketing the camouflage phase let me consider anything girly (the word alone leaving a sour taste in my mouth at that age), but this fledgeling effort to be in congruity with my surroundings was a truer form of camouflage than those country garments.

Adaptive, as in nature, this camouflage moulded itself around my anxiety. That instinctive need to bear resemblance to one's surroundings became instead a desire for invisibility, like the fish that become part of the scenery. My disguise was never quite as seamless. It slipped with every lapse in confidence, a long-running bluff revealed in many cornered moments. Red face, shaking hands, shaking voice – all of them betraying too clearly the message I sought to communicate to the world. *I Am Not Here.*

I like to think that I don't need that protective camouflage anymore. Blending into the background is second nature. Not a way to hide, but a way to watch life from the sidelines, participating in it when I choose to. No more clenched fists or breathless silences: my anxiety has morphed into something closer to apathy; introversion.

Still, that old chant returns sometimes. When I am thrust into the foreground and people's eyes on me are like individual chisels, or when I am only imagining that they are. At parties. Public speaking. Backed into a corner I shrink into myself as if I could disappear into it.

When cuttlefish are placed in front of chequered wallpaper they adopt its colours but not its pattern. There are no right angles in nature, and so they can only create blobs of black across their whitened flesh, at odds with their surroundings. I think of how I press myself against the nearest wall at gatherings, too tense to appear natural. My body is all right angles, all straight-edged awkward limbs that I am all too aware of. Too conscious of the fact that *I Am Here.*

I need something to clench my fists around, and find a drink to disappear into, softening my edges.

I am still envious of that child layered in forest colours.

* * *

Searching the hangers for my winter coat today, I find a rumpled jacket. I haven't seen it since the last time it was dug up and donned over my old rotation of baggy, form-hiding shirts, paired with heavy boots and unskilled eyeliner. It is the sole survivor of the camouflage purge – mostly because it was borrowed from my mother. I bring it out to the light and touch the studded design on its back, redolent of the biker rallies at which it was bought.

Its disjointed mess of dull, green-brown shades have been tinged with embarrassment for me since my camouflage year. A time recalled incredulously by those who knew me then.

I think of the self who was shrouded in the garish print without restraint or regard for appearances; without reason.

I put it on. Not with that childhood confidence but with something closer to it than I had in those intervening years.

A facsimile of the feeling. A whiff of smoke in the face.

An Elegy for a Box

Emily Walker

The wooden box on her mantelpiece was stained with
echoes of her paper-thin fingertips
tapping the lid,

lingering in the dust. The lid arched like her back
and the box was engraved in gold
which matched

the mustard fade-marks on the Persian rug. I grazed
my finger across the wood, the lines
like veins,

touching her history, I felt too near. I was standing
where she once stood, not dusting
the cabinet or feeding

the plant. I remembered the earrings she kept in there,
imagining their weight, next to
the strand of hair

she kept in a handkerchief. Her mantelpiece fossils
left their dust silhouettes like
some colossal

nuclear bomb, leaving ash-shadow residents
on the shelf. These were the
surviving remnants,

the smoke barely cleared, crackling still audible,
surrounding me. I longed for
something intangible.

Give me her myths, the fables spanning decades
of working in a factory during
distant air-raids,

the sirens too far away to hear. But not the box,
which deafened me with her laugh, and
brought her back.

first memories

Carl Walsh

first memories   my journey began wide-eyed in innocence sun splaying golden light across drunken wheatfield heads intoxicating under red harvester blade as real as fireworks displacing far-off cosmos of darkness & light in shatter of colour wheeling overhead these dreams foment this being underpin the whole as real as summer scented grass crushed underfoot a caravanserai caught in passing of days that trip endlessly forward rain spilling down round Neolithic mounds to drain in chalk fields & run on in rivulets forming underground   echoes   of   forgotten   self unseen   but   flowing unstoppable & endless beneath

these contours of change

Quiet flows the Hull

Clint Wastling

I can see Beverley Minster across the ings.
Towers of magnesian limestone
glimpsed between trees across
Flatlands that ancestors tilled.

Great John, magnified through air's prism,
chimes the hour
as it has since 1901.
Heard by four generations, now gone.

No place a shadow can hide
under the sun, where the Hull flows
silver, sometimes sapphire,
often grey under a sodden sky.

Old willows feel the tug of tides,
roots securing the banks, holding fast.
Our roots secure, becoming entwined
with each ebb and flow of the river.

The carillon's peel carried east
across the ings. A song ancestors heard
as they tilled these fields, toiled,
aware of their here, their now.

Whalebones

Indee Watson

Seagulls bow to the
Whalebones of Whitby,
their cries curling round
ivory bone in
blissful harmony;
A crowd singing their
gratitude for the
bed of blue.

I was small,
too small to paddle
in the murky depths,
lest my little body sink far
below the surface,
and the waves wash away
the memory of me.
So I settled
for rockpools.

Soon I grew taller and
the sea sang out,
her lullabies sweet in
the summer air.
I drew nearer and the
horizon distorted,
thick with sea salt
and forgotten days.

Her rippling waves
retreated as she inhaled,
to uncover a collation
of treasures,
sea glass and shells
carved deep
into the sand.

I inhaled to uncover
my longing for her
deep waters.

She sings to me now,
each note lingering in
the air, an echo
of her melodic past,
her tune fading
into obscurity across
her infinite shores.

I run
along peppering sand
and jagged pebbles,
my doubts sprinkled along the
shoreline like bread
for the ducks,
as the sea whisks them
far away from here.

She washes away
the memory of my troubles,
painting them into her horizon
as I look on from the
Whalebones of Whitby.

Returning Home

Lorraine Wood

Frozen beaks like ivory coated on the window sill outside, glass beads stare back. The icy metal bucket of tadpoles waits for spring. Black and white memories like scuffed shoe polish on newspaper. A tide mark in the bowl.

Blinds and shutters now block out the light.

The sound of the trains still lingers into the sidings, coal trains long gone. Dust hangs like midges in the air. Moggies squat on the back wall waiting for bin day to fight over scraps and bones, wail and hiss until they've had their fill. Mum chases them with the yard brush and a bucket of soapy water.

I keep walking back to the same street with its black and white paintwork and front door.

10 Harcourt Street.

My heart scratched into the red brick.

I see three brass monkeys, bald heads shine from my constant polishing. My fingers thick with the smell of *Brasso* seeped into their bodies, melded together, lingered under their noses.

Bleach. Disinfectant, on floors and in our bath, sanitised us.

But this was home.

I see the cord mat where my brother grazed his chin, falling from his chair after rocking back and forth. The coal fire in the back kitchen of the terraced house where I was born.

I grew accustomed to the feeling
of the cord wrapped securely
around my neck. Colouring
me a tingling shade of blue.

The midwifes safe hands
detached me, blade swished
cold steel tugged my wired
lifeline. The door slammed

firmly shut, rattling the letter
box as Dad left for work.

I gave an awkward cry
drowned out by distant fireworks
the day before bonfire night.

Crackling spitting wood and objects Mum positions between fire-lighters.

They ignite new flames, burning orange embers sink deeper into the night.

I see Mum's strong hands shield us from the flames as she pushes yesterday's newspaper up the chimney. I could hear the siren close by.

The brass handle of the little brush as I sweep the fallen ash.

Remnants of the past lay lifeless by morning.

The red back gate, paint curled at the bottom like the hem of a skirt puckered like an old skin.

Echoes from the tin bath as the train leaves its sidings, replenished with coal and nutty-slack.

My hands dig deep searching for the tiniest speck of gold, my fingers half-bitten by the dust of kings. The water drains, splashing the yard and neatly edged moss, a milky grey water from the bath were my brother had left the soap in too long, holding its breath as a stream of bubbles floated and popped.

Mum the centre of our universe, but she was more than this.

Her eyes sparkled like indigo smudged on my watercolour palette.

Her hands strong as if a sculptor had left behind some clay, they warmed and moulded me.

Her bubbly permed hair kept reminders of her past neatly rolled into curls.

Her glasses scattered with stains that only she could see through.

Her laugh I grew up with, a string of harmonies, an infectious cure for any ailment.

Her crimpolene dress I left an iron-shaped tattoo on.

Her cocktail gown, silk, I'd get lost in the colours of the world.

Her rules she stuck to like treacle toffee apples she made for the street.

Her ability to sew, knit, create a world for us, a childhood without any spare change.

Her grief for her mum from the age of nine was a raw onion she couldn't peel.

Her scent, perfumes that followed us to adulthood, heavy drops of memories.

Her courage was oceans teaching us to swim deep and far.

Her sense of humour she had borrowed from her dad. A funny blend she gave us like bags of sweets divvied out on a rainy days.

Her devotion was priceless, she loved unconditionally, clung to us through every pore.

She was the needle in a sewing machine whizzing through every corner of the garment of our days.

She suffered like the pleats of a skirt pressed into submission. Heat exposed the fibres of her heart, her body ravaged, savaged by a disease too raw to imagine, stripping her emotions bare like the red flock wallpaper that sat above the fireplace: nobody home.

My family drifts, exists, travelling but going nowhere. Roots still linger under the cobbles in the alleyway.

I can't take the bus without seeing into the eyes of strangers a painful lingering of something I cannot reach.

I cannot take the bus without a song on my iPod reminding me, surrounding me with a pain so deep it suffocates me, churns me up and spits me onto the pavement at my destination.

The beach.

A bucketful of sand and water, remnants of the tide.

Colourful summers. Sunday best.

A place to exist for the day.

I loved the sand, but not the sea, nor the seaweed wrapping itself around my ankles, like brown beads.

Sand and paste filled sandwiches and the cockles we called ducks.

The things we once had, now lay hidden in the ottoman at the bottom of the bed, filled with crisp white sheets and embroidered table cloths, and strands of hair curled into a velvet box, lies in the arms of dried weeds.

Lives unpicked, threads of nature, stitched to repair the wounds of skin, and open hearts of the war. A battle to belong.

Loss.

…is like emptying the bath while your world is struggling to escape the suds and the tide marks that your brother left from his mechanical job.

What I would give for 'War of the Worlds' to be beating its wings against the net curtain of the open window of the living room, and Mum letting him turn the volume up, because she could, but

I liked 'Delilah', Tom Jones crooning to his heart's content, and Mum's 'Porgy and Bess' when nobody was listening.

Memories

The missing button on your coat when you were five.

The missing button on your coat now.

Finding the way to belong is like searching for your button among the cobbled streets of your childhood.

Returning home.

Author Biographies

Peter Arnds

Peter Arnds directs the Comparative Literature programme at Trinity College Dublin. He is a member of PEN International and of Academia Europaea. His publications include books on Günter Grass, the Holocaust, and *Wolves at the Door: Migration, Dehumanization, Rewilding the World* (Bloomsbury, 2021). Peter is the translator of the Swiss novel *Stromschnellen* (Rapids, Dalkey Archive Press, nominated for IMPAC, the Dublin International Literary Award) and published many stories and poems in journals such as Cyphers (Dublin), pendora magazine, glossen, and in Dedalus Press. His novel *Searching for Alice* (Dalkey Archive Press, 2018) is currently being made into an audiobook.

Chris Bailey

Chris Bailey is a busy person. He is an educator, filmmaker, musician, artist and writer. After spending the past decade making artist film and commercial documentaries, he has recently returned to writing. *The Funeral Coat* is his first published writing. Chris is a founding member of Imperfect Orchestra, an experimental community music project and is a Senior Lecturer in BA (Hons) Film and Screen Arts at Plymouth College of Art. He lives in Devon with his wife, Erin, and son, Jackson.

Anna Boyle

Anna Lives in a small town in Yorkshire near to the 'Gateway to the Dales'. Having a number of interests including family, walking and being a keen craft hobbyist, she has also always had a love of the written word. Study of literature at school fanned the flames of an avid reading habit started in her early years, and later encouraged a desire to write. Anna is a member of a U3A writing group and has worked through a creative writing course. She is currently studying an online non-fiction course. In April one of Anna's creative non-fiction stories was published online with Storyhouse (Preservation Foundation Inc.).

Beth Brooke

Beth Brooke is a retired teacher, born in the Middle East but now living in Dorset, close to the stunning Jurassic Coast. Its chalk landscape and the desert landscape of her childhood inspire and influence her writing. Her debut collection, *A Landscape With Birds* will be published by Hedgehog Press in 2022. She has poems in a number of online journals and print anthologies. She can be found on Twitter as @BethBrooke8.

Elinor Clark

Elinor Clark is originally from Leeds and now lives and studies in Germany. She enjoys writing and performing poetry, chatting about philosophy, coding and vegan steak bakes. Her work has recently appeared or is forthcoming in journals including *The Blue Nib Literary Magazine, The London Magazine, Marble Poetry* and *Poetry Birmingham*, and she was a featured poet in the erbacce 2020 prize.

Shelley Corcoran

Shelley Corcoran has had her poetry published in Murze Magazine (https://www.murze.org/), issues 11 and 12 and Life in Lockdown Exhibition (Library Association of Ireland). Shelley's poetry has also appeared in *A New Ulster Literary Magazine, The Galway Review 9 Anthology, Parentheses Journal, Tír na nÓg Literary Mag* and *Green Ink Poetry, Collection 5*. Her work will appear in four anthologies for publication summer 2021, *Shadow of the Past, Nostalgia, Cut the Crap* and *The Unsung Melodies.*

Lucy Crispin

Lucy Crispin is a former Poet Laureate of South Cumbria and has been published widely in print and online, most recently in *Cake, Speckled Trout, Anthropocene, Pennine Platform* and *Channel*. A passionate believer in shared reading, she facilitates poetry-based groups and works freelance for the Wordsworth Trust; she also loves performing. You can find information about forthcoming events and access past performances at lucycrispin.com, where you can also find her regular poetry column. Her pamphlets *wish you were here* and *shades of blue* were published in 2020 by Hedgehog Press.

Tash J Curry

Tash is an aspiring non binary transgender writer, poet from York. They started pursuing writing at seventeen and found a way of turning feelings into words as a form of therapy. When studying at York St John University they published a few pieces of creative writing and poetry, they include *Maybe. Just Maybe, But I Guess Somethings are Better Left Unsaid, Our Tragic Ends, Name One Hero Who Was Happy* and *Fate's Game*. They also have a current poetry blog under the name – Tash Writes on wordpress.

Joseph Darlington

Joseph Darlington is a writer from Manchester, UK. He was nominated for the Dinesh Allirajah Prize for Short Fiction in 2018. He is co-editor of the *Manchester Review of Books*. His latest book, *Quiz Night*, a play-along-at-home novel about pub quizzing, is available from www.josefadarlington.co.uk.

He is on Twitter at @Joe_Darlo.

Sarah Davy

Sarah Davy is a writer and facilitator living and working in rural Northumberland. Her short fiction is published online and in print and her first short play, *A Perfect Knot*, was performed at Newcastle Theatre Royal in 2020. Sarah was shortlisted for the Northern Writers Awards in 2020. She was commissioned by Hexham Book Festival in 2020 and was writer in residence at Forum Books in Corbridge for 2019-2020. Sarah is working on her first novel and a collection of essays exploring belonging in rural communities.

RC deWinter

RC deWinter's poetry is widely anthologized, notably in *Uno: A Poetry Anthology* (Xlibris, April 2002), *New York City Haiku* (Universe/NY Times, February 2017), *Coffin Bell Two* (Coffin Bell, March 2020) *Winter Anthology: Healing Felines and Femmes,* (Other Worldly Women Press, December 2020), Now We Heal: An Anthology of Hope, (Wellworth Publishing, December 2020) in print in *2River, Adelaide, Door Is A Jar, Event Magazine, Gargoyle Magazine, Genre Urban Arts, Gravitas, Kansas City Voices, Meat For Tea: The Valley Review, the minnesota review, Night Picnic Journal, Prairie Schooner, Reality Break Press, Southword,* among others and appears in numerous online literary journals.

Peter J Donnelly

Peter J Donnelly lives in York where he works as a hospital secretary. He has degrees in English and Creative Writing from the University of Wales Lampeter. He has been published in several magazines and anthologies. He was a joint runner up in the Buzzwords Open Poetry Competition with his poem 'The Second of August' and was commended in the Poetry Kit Competition with his entry 'Seagulls'.

Scott Elder

Scott Elder lives in France. His work has been published in the UK, Ireland, and abroad. A debut pamphlet, *Breaking Away,* was published by Poetry Salzburg in 2015; a first collection, *Part of the Dark,* by Dempsey&Windle 2017 (UK), and his second, *My Hotel,* is forthcoming from Salmon Poetry 2023 (Ireland).

Nathaniel Frankland

Born in 1994, Nathaniel Frankland is a proud Yorkshireman currently residing in London. After reading French at University, he now works in the wine trade, using his free time to write poetry and songs. Nathaniel takes inspiration from things we overlook and take for granted, endeavouring to explain their wider significance in our lives.

Jeremy Gadd

Jeremy Gadd has previously contributed over 300 poems in literary magazines and periodicals in Australia, the USA, the UK, Canada, New Zealand, Germany, Belgium, Malaya and India. He has MA Honours and PhD degrees from the University of New England and his writing has won several literary awards. He lives and writes in an old Federation era house overlooking Botany Bay, the birthplace of modern Australia. Further information can be found at: https://jeremygaddpoet.com.

Victoria Gatehouse

Victoria Gatehouse is a poet and medical researcher. Her poems have been published in many magazines including *The North, Poetry News, Magma, Mslexia* and *The Rialto* and broadcast on BBC radio. Competition wins include Iklley, Otley and PENfro. Victoria's second pamphlet, *The Mechanics of Love*, published by smith|doorstop, was a Laureate's Choice for 2019.

Elizabeth Gibson

Elizabeth Gibson is a Manchester writer and performer whose work explores city life, queerness, community, mental health, nature and folklore. She won a Northern Writers' Award in 2017, and received a DYCP grant in 2021 from Arts Council England to develop her writing and performance. Her work has appeared in journals such as *404 Ink, Atrium, Confingo, Ink, Sweat & Tears, Litro, Popshot* and *Strix*. In 2020, she was chosen to represent Manchester City of Literature in Tartu, Estonia with her poem 'Arrival' shared on bus windows there.

She blogs at http://elizabethgibsonwriter.blogspot.com and Tweets and Instagrams as @Grizonne.

Daniel Hinds

Daniel Hinds won the Poetry Society's Timothy Corsellis Young Critics Prize. His poetry has been published or is forthcoming in *The London Magazine, The New European, Wild Court, Stand, The*

Best New British and Irish Poets 2019-2021, Poetry Birmingham, Blackbox Manifold, The Honest Ulsterman, Finished Creatures, Rewilding: An Ecopoetic Anthology, Perverse, Riggwelter, The Seventh Quarry, New Contrast, and elsewhere. He has been commissioned by New Creatives, a talent development scheme supported by Arts Council England and BBC Arts and delivered by Tyneside Cinema, to produce an audio piece based on his poetic sequence *The Stone Men of Newcastle.* Twitter: @DanielGHinds.

Neil James Hudson

Neil James Hudson has published around fifty fantasy and science fiction stories. He is currently working on a story cycle entitled *One Hundred Pieces of Millia Maslowa* (which includes *As Beautiful Things Always Do*) and a short novel about the imaginary city of Belkot. He recently obtained a distinction in the Creative Writing MA programme at York St John University and works as a charity shop manager in York. When not writing he is often to be found in art galleries looking at weird stuff.

Beth Kilkenny

Beth Kilkenny writes short fiction and personal essays. She has an MA in Literary Studies. Beth has been published in *The Blue Nib Literary Magazine, Selcouth Station, BlueHouse Journal and Lunate.* Beth was a participant in the MumWrite experimental writing development programme funded by Arts Council England. She is from Newcastle Upon Tyne.

David Linklater

David Ross Linklater is a poet from Balintore, Easter Ross. He is the author of three pamphlets, most recently *Scenes from a God Movie* (Speculative Books, 2021). He was shortlisted for the 2020 Edwin Morgan Award and is the recipient of a Dewar Arts Award. His work has appeared in *Bath Magg, New Writing Scotland* and *Gutter,* amongst others. He lives and writes in Glasgow. Twitter: @DavidRossLinkla www.davidlinklaterpoetry.com

James McDermott

James McDermott's plays published by Samuel French include *Rubber Ring* and *Time and Tide*. Their poetry collection *Manatomy* is published by Burning Eye and their forthcoming pamphlet *Eraised* will be published by Polari Press. James's poems have been published in various magazines including *The Gay and Lesbian Review, The Cardiff Review, Popshot Quarterly, Ink Sweat and Tears, Spelt, Dreich, Confluence, Bitchin' Kitsch, The Adriatic* and *Dawntreader*. James was shortlisted for Outspoken's Performance Poetry Prize 2020 and Commended in The Winchester Poetry Prize 2020 judged by Andrew McMillan.

Lucinda Morton

Lucy Morton is a third year Creative Writing and English Literature student at York St John University, graduating in summer 2021. She is originally from Cheshire, and thoroughly enjoys works exploring reflection and introspection. Her poetry was published in both the 2020 and 2021 editions of the *Beyond the Walls* anthology, and was also part of the Crossed Lines *Dial-a-Poem* project, for which her poem 'The Quiet Noise' was commended.

Alicia Sometimes

Alicia Sometimes is a poet, writer and broadcaster. She has performed her spoken word and poetry at many venues, festivals and events around the world. Her poems have been in Best Australian Science Writing, Best Australian Poems and many more. She is director/co-writer of the art/science planetarium shows, *Elemental* and *Particle/Wave*. Her TedxUQ talk in 2019 was about the passion of combining art with science.

Claire Urquhart

Claire grew up in Carnoustie, Scotland. A product of the 80s Scottish education system, where decent exam results and a fear of blood meant she ended up studying law in Edinburgh where she now lives. It took her 15 years to escape from law and find her way back to her first love: literature, and especially poetry. She co-founded a charity (Open Book) that uses literature as a way to connect people and communities. She writes whenever she gets the chance, which more often than not at the moment, is in the dead of night.

Cheyenne Uustal

Cheyenne Uustal currently studies Creative Writing at York St John University. She is a poet and fictional writer who enjoys experimenting with her style and genre. After a lifetime of being passionate about writing, she has always aspired to get published. Her first publication was of a poem when she was just seven years old but her most recent are some articles she wrote for *Mindless Mag.*

Lydia Waites

Lydia Waites is an East Yorkshire based writer and Creative Writing PhD student at the University of Lincoln. She is the Editor-in-Chief of Tether's End Magazine and former fiction editor for *The Lincoln Review.* Her work has been appeared in *Door Is A Jar, The Abandoned Playground,* and *FEED.* Find her at @lydiawaiteswrites on Instagram or @waites_lydia on Twitter, or being dragged around the Wolds by a springer spaniel.

Emily Walker

Emily Walker was born in York and now resides in a disconcertingly quiet village outside Tadcaster. She is currently studying an MA in Creative Writing with York St John University, has a degree in English Literature from Durham University and a PGCE in Secondary English from York University. Her writing has been published in *Ellipsis Zine, Sink Magazine* and the *Beyond the Walls* 2021 anthology, and she has recently been longlisted for the TSS Publishing BIFFY50 Microfiction Competition.

Carl Walsh

Carl is an Australian poet, crossword compiler, lexicographer of fictional words, writer of horoscopes and other fairy stories. His work has been published in *StylusLit, n-SCRIBE, Cordite Poetry Review, Meniscus, Rabbit, Plumwood Mountain, Australian Poetry Journal, Verity La, Southerly, Meanjin, takahe, Cha: an Asian Literary Journal* and *Tokyo Poetry Review*. He's also had haiku published in *Wales Haiku Journal, Kokako* and *Echidna Tracks* (forthcoming). His mother is originally from Bury, near Manchester, and his first memories are of going to England around the time he turned three. As he nears fifty, he thought this a suitable topic for 'Time and Memory'.

Clint Wastling

Clint Wastling's poetry has been published in *Orbis, Spelt* and *Consilience* amongst other magazines. Clint has a collection called *Layers* published by Maytree Press. His novel, *The Geology of Desire*, is an LGBTQ thriller set around Whitby in the 1980's and Hull during World War II. He also has a sci-fi novel: *Tyrants Rex* set 3000 years in the future, both are published by Stairwell Books.

Indee Watson

Indee Watson is a writer from Pudsey, studying creative writing at York St John University. Her writing ranges from poetry to short stories, haikus to novels, and has been published in works such as *Neutral Magazine* and *Beyond the Walls*. Though her fiction has a strong focus on the dark and macabre, her poetry often takes inspiration from landscapes, particularly the sea. Her writing, both poetry and fiction, strives to portray the beautiful Northern landscapes in which she writes.

Lorraine Wood

Lorraine is a mature student studying at the University of Salford doing a part-time practice-based Creative writing PhD. She has previously completed a BA (Hons) Creative writing at Liverpool

John Moores University and an MA in Creative writing at University of Chester. She has two grown up children and a three-year-old grandson. She has been included in local anthologies, and been shortlisted and placed for poetry competitions in the past. Poetry is her first love, and she is working on a collection of poetry for her PhD, which involves many different approaches to writing poetry through style and themes, unusual and surreal at times.

Acknowledgements

The York Literary Review 2021 Team would like to thank Dr Rob O'Connor for all of his work with the very first Publishing MA course at York St John University, in connection with the York Centre for Writing. Thank you to Jamie McGarry at Valley Press for all of his help teaching the team. We would like to thank the York St John community, which has shaped many of our own stories and memories, as well as continuing to inspire us in these current times. We would also like to mention Leanne Roberts for her assistance with the celebration event. Thank you to all of our friends and family, we appreciate you all! Of course, a huge thank you goes to all of this year's contributors, as well as to everyone who sent in submissions! Without all of you, the 2021 edition of the York Literary Review would not have been possible.